I Wish I Had Known My Father

Barry Scott Crisp.

Introduction.

The Miners strike in 1984 didn't just hurt the mining industry and those that worked in the industry. It hurt whole communities and tore out the heart of these communities. Friends and Families turning their wrath on each other as the strike bit into the finances of the families. Government was the enemy but yet the community turned on itself causing years of anger. What happened to those babies born at the start of that strike? They had no say and had no knowledge of what struggles were ahead.
Helen and Joan were two such babies who were eighteen years of age and the future of the communities could be in the hands of them and their age groups.

Helen and Joan are now twenty one years of age Helen's grandmother died in 2004 only managing two years of trying to get to know her long lost granddaughter.

This is a story that gives thought to people and their lives affected by some actions that were not even their responsibility and yet their lives were changed forever.

Chapter One.

Helen Taylor was eighteen years old and had been moved from one foster home to another for as long as she could remember. Her only recollections of her parents were from photographs and flash backs in her dreams. Every time that she had approached the subject with her different foster parents they always avoided giving her what she was seeking. In fact as she grew older she had come to realise that she needed to know more if her life was to go forward.

Since 2000 she had lived in a home for young girls just outside Doncaster. She was moved to this place on her sixteenth birthday she never had understood the reasons for this. She tried asking why they had insisted that she leave the home that she had come to like.

She had been happy there she had been fostered into that home for almost eight years and had made some new friends.

These were the sort of decisions that made Helen nervous and unsure whenever the social services visited her. In her mind she blamed herself for being moved and no one tried to tell her any different.

She had been worried about her future when they moved her to this place that they called Homelands. How long would she be staying here she missed the talks that she had with her previous foster mothers, as this seemed more like a school and no one sat in the cosiness of a front room and listened to what she had to say.

One good thing had come from her move to Homelands in that Helen had made a friend a good friend. This was something new to Helen because relationships had not been one of her strong points. She had become withdrawn due the number of times that she had moved from one home to another. This caused her not to bother making friends because she could not simply see the point of it.

At first Helen was dubious about this girl when she approached her as they walked around the extensive grounds that surrounded Homelands. She introduced herself as Joan Fields she was of similar age to Helen and had come to Homelands in 2001. She came from a village in Yorkshire called Grimethorpe. Joan asked Helen if she knew the place but Helen just shook her head.

Joan saw in Helen a person that she could trust and she needed someone to confide in and guessed that Helen would have similar needs. They began to talk more but Helen was still acting reserved not daring to allow this girl to get too close.

The weeks and months passed and they gradually became closer and closer and started to laugh with each other.

Helen was a true blonde haired girl with lovely blue eyes and Joan had red hair and green eyes. This was one of the many things that made them laugh together. They had heard many stories about girls with blonde and red hair but they hadn't felt like any of these stories.

Over the weeks they each told the other about their lives before they came to Homelands.

Joan told Helen how at the age of ten she was involved with her parents in an accident when they were travelling to Blackpool on her very first holiday in the summer of 1993. Her mother was killed and her father was seriously injured so much so that he was unable to work anymore.

Helen had tears in her eyes and was thinking how brave her friend Joan was being and wondered if she would be as brave if she spoke about her life. Helen asked Joan why she did not live with her father anymore. Joan wiped the tears from her eyes and softly replied to Helen's question.

"He could not carry on after mother died. Oh he tried so hard but he kept breaking down and his legs became worse so that he was in a wheelchair all the time. I was too young to care for him and although he tried so hard they had to take him into a home."

"What happened to you then?"

Again Joan sat quiet and slowly moved her hands over her eyes to wipe away the tears. This was the first time that she had opened up and had not realised how upset she had been inside where all this had been bottled up.

"At first they sent me to one of my auntie's to stay whilst my father got better. It was all right but she already had four children of her own and I was upset all of the time and I think that she felt she could not cope. I stayed there for about six months but then she became ill and I had to move. I was placed with a couple in the next village they were called foster parents. I had never heard of such people before. I tell you I was really worried about this and I almost ran away but where could I have gone?"

Helen shook her head in acknowledgement.

Both sat there in silence for a moment. They were both locked into their early lives and Helen could see very similar periods in her life that Joan had in hers'.

Joan stood up and asked Helen if they could have a walk.

It was a bright summer's day and the sun seemed to help when spirits were low. The grounds were quite extensive and many offers had been made to those that owned Homelands to allow some development within the grounds for new houses perhaps to house some of the residents of Homelands in later life.

This reason for the development was seen as just a ploy to get their feet under the table. They would then make money from the development not for the benefit of those they said were their intentions. Neither spoke for a while but they felt the comfort and the relaxing feeling that the warmth of the sun gave them.

They came to a large oak tree that took central position in the grounds and had been there for longer than anyone could remember. They sat on a seat that had been given to the home by one of the residents from many years ago.

Helen was the first to open the conversation. She commented on the oak tree and she asked Joan what sights this tree must have seen throughout its life.

"It must be at least two hundred years old I wonder who walked these grounds then. I bet this place was full of magnificent trees like this. You can imagine the nobility that rode their fine horses through these woods. How times have changed. It makes you realise what insignificance we are when you look up at this tree."

Joan looked at Helen. "Yes but I think that we may not have the significance of this tree but we have an important place in this world. We just have to find out why we have been placed here and then perhaps we then could understand better."

Helen shook her head. "I wish that I could just have known my father."

Joan took hold of Helen's shoulder and squeezed. "You never knew your father then? What about your mother where was she in your life? Is she dead?"

Helen sat quiet her chin sank into her neck.

Joan gave her time to come to terms with her question.

"I can remember a little about a lady but I am not sure whether she was my mother. I once saw a photograph where this lady was holding a baby. I was told that I was that baby the lady could have been anyone so I am not sure if she was my mother. If she is still alive I am not sure but I have asked but no one would tell me."

"Why don't we try and find out then? We could do it together, that is if you want to."

Helen gazed across at her friend. She had often thought of trying to find out but was too nervous and frightened to start. Rejection was something that she had felt all of her life and was not sure how she would be able to handle it if it happened now.

"Would you help me Joan?"

"Of course I would that is what friends do they help each other?"

"When can we start?"

"It is not when it is where. We have to have something to go on, some facts about your early years that gives us some direction on this journey of discovery into your life. Can you remember anything?"

"I still have that photograph I told you about but I don't know if that will help. Other than that I have the name and address of my last foster parents maybe they could help us."

"Well that is a start."

"What about you though Joan? What about your father?"

Joan's eyes filled with tears once again.

Helen quickly took hold of her. "I am so sorry if I have upset you Joan. I just meant…

"It's all right Helen don't worry I am just being silly."

Quietness fell across both of the girls. Helen just looked at her friend and knew that at last she had someone that she could feel close to.

Joan sniffed up and told Helen that her father was in a hospital. He had lost any sense of reality and didn't even know her when she visited him.

"Oh I am so sorry Joan I didn't know. I didn't mean to pry I knew that you were so close to your father."

"Well yes he was such a proud man and very strong on principles. In fact he used to drive my mother mad with his pride and his principles. Sometimes I would hear them arguing about something or other. They often disagreed on the principles that my father thought were so important. His pride though was his cornet playing in the colliery band. He loved that they were very good in those days winning competitions. I believed that that the band meant more to him than me or my mother."

Helen looked towards Joan. "I can't think that would be true Joan. He sounded like a father any girl would be proud to have. I know that I would and I believe that principles are so important Joan. I don't think that life would be the same without us all having some principles."

"I agree but he would take them to the eleventh degree and was like a bulldog he just would not let go. The doctors believe that this is one of the reasons why his mind could not cope with his incapacity and drove him into the state that he is today."

"How often do you visit him then?"

"Not as much as I should but it get so upset and that does not help him or me so I just keep away. Inside I do feel terrible but……."

"I can understand that Joan, really I can."

"Thank you but it does not help my internal sadness."

They stood up from the seat under the large oak tree and walked back towards the home. Teatime was approaching and although the sun was still shining there was freshness in the air and neither had any cover over their shoulders.

Joan suddenly had a thought. "Do you think that Mrs. Freeman could help us?"

Mrs. Freeman was the principle of Homelands and she should have some of the backgrounds of all the girls that were in the home.

"I never thought of that Joan. Do you think that she would tell us I am not sure how these things work? There's always been some secrecy about adoptions and fostering I don't know why."

"Well there are new laws now that means that children have the right to know who their parents are so she can't really refuse."

"Well we can only ask she can only say no. I hope that she doesn't I don't know if I could take that."

They walked back towards the house and there was something exciting had moved into their steps just in a matter of hours.

Helen took hold of Joan's hand and gave it a squeeze.

They ate their tea with much more vigour than usual that night. Both of them looked towards the top table where the principal Mrs. Freeman was sat.

They could not help thinking how she would react when they asked her questions about Helen's background.

They started to snigger at some of the thoughts that they were having and those sat close by looked shocked at the sudden change in these two girls that had showed no signs of anything like these before.

After tea that night they went to Helen's room and sat down on her bed. This was the first time that anyone had been allowed in her room but she felt comfortable about it.

"Right let's have a look at that photograph Helen. If we are to talk to the principal then we need to rehearse the questions that we want answers to. If we go in without any plan we will come out regretting the lost opportunity."

Helen took shoebox from out of her small wardrobe and laid it on the bed. Removing the lid Joan glanced over trying to see what else Helen had in the shoebox. Finally Helen lifted the photograph out of the box and looked down at it before handing it to Joan.

"She is beautiful whoever the lady is Helen. It must be your mother you have her eyes and around the mouth. Yes I would be surprised if she is not related to you in some form or other."

"Do you think so Joan?" Helen felt a sudden tinge of excitement flow through her body. Could she really be my mother?

They spent the next few hours setting out some of the questions that Helen should ask Mrs. Freeman. Joan looked at the small wall clock that hung over Helen's bed. "Look at the time Helen. Ten o'clock I must go."

Helen and Joan rose off the bed and Helen took hold of Joan and pulled into a hug.

"Thank you Joan."

"I have not done anything as yet."

"Oh yes you have. You have become my friend something that I have never felt for what seems to be all of my life. Thank you for that. When do you feel that I should approach Mrs. Freeman?"

"Why not tomorrow there is not much point in putting off the evil day, as the saying goes. I don't know why they felt that it was an evil day. If things go as we hope it could be the start of a journey of joy especially for you".

"I do hope so Joan, I do hope so. I can't help feeling very nervous about the whole thing."

"Mrs. Freeman is not a bad person Helen. I think I hope that she sees that this information is so important to you. I think that when you see her tomorrow I think that she will be very helpful."

"When she sees me tomorrow I thought that you would be there with me."

"Why do you want me there?"

"Now there is a daft question Joan. I don't think that I could face her by myself. I would stammer and stutter. God I don't think that I can do it, not alone anyway."

"I think that you could but if you fell that strongly about it of course I will come along. I was just thinking that you would want to hear what she had to say alone. I didn't want to intrude."

"Intrude if it wasn't for you and your help I would never have had the courage to even start. No you have a great deal to do with this."

"All right Helen I will come."

They both started to laugh Helen laughed due to the fact that Joan had agreed to come. Hers was a very nervous laugh more than one of happiness. Helen hardly slept that night as she rehearsed her conversation with Mrs. Freeman. Then she thought about the fact what if she refused to talk to me. She has to talk to me; she must talk to me. This argument went through her mind until she suddenly woke up next morning not knowing that she had actually fallen to sleep. Her eyes seemed heavy through what she thought was, the lack of a good night's sleep.

She took a shower and put on her clothes. She and Joan had free periods first thing and that would be the best opportunity to try and speak to Mrs. Freeman. The next hour or so would seem to be a lifetime before they were actually sat down…. Would they be invited to sit down or would she just tell them to get out of her office.

Joan and Helen met at breakfast and silence seemed to be the need at that moment. They both had their minds fixed on the next hour and the approach they would have to make to Mrs. Freeman. Breakfast over and some of the girls left for their first classes. Helen would normally walk along to the library and find a book to read until her first period. On this occasion however they both walked in the direction of Mrs. Freeman's office. Still they never spoke not until they were about three strides from the dark wooden door that was the entrance to Mrs. Freeman's office. They stopped looked at each other and gave a glint of a smile.

"Here we go Helen."

They were just about to knock on the door when it swung open and there stood Mrs. Freeman. Suddenly she looked more menacing than they had imagined all the time that had been at Homelands.

"Hello girls did you want to see me?"

Helen and Joan stood there for a moment although they tried to speak no words came forth.

"Well girls?"

Helen felt the excitement return and before she had realised what she was doing she gave the reply to the question that they had been asked.

"Yes we need to see you on a personal note Mrs. Freeman. Joan, Miss Fields is just here as a friend. I want her with me, if that is all right with you?"

"That will be fine Helen but I am not sure what it is that you want from me. I suggest that you come in to my office and then I may have a better understanding. Go on in me will be there in a moment I just have to see… Well go in and take a seat I will be about five minutes."

Helen and Joan both blew out their cheeks having passed the first hurdle. They entered the office in fact both had ever been in there before and were shocked at the size. It was much smaller that they had imagined but quite cosy.

They sat in two chairs that stood either side of the small but neatly laid out desk. Neither of them spoke both filled with their own thoughts and both feeling very nervous at the prospect of what may happen in the next half- hour or so.

The occasional smile across the desk trying to help calm the nerves they just sat and waited for the return of Mrs. Freeman.

Chapter Two.

The clock on the wall above the desk told Helen that Mrs. Freeman should be due back very soon and this did nothing to help her nerves. Her palms on her hands were wet with perspiration she took out a handkerchief and tried to wipe them dry.
The door suddenly opened startling both of them. They immediately stood up out of the chairs.
Mrs. Freeman smiled and bid them good morning. She told them to sit down and then started to shuffle some papers on her desk before looking silently at both girls.
"Now then Helen what was it that you felt was so important to see me about? You said that it was a personal thing I believe."
Helen felt as though she was about to choke but coughed to relieve the uncomfortable feeling in her throat.

"Yes Mrs. Freeman it is a personal thing and I wondered if you could help me with…."

"Excuse me a moment Helen if it is a personal item why is it that Joan here is sitting in with us?"

"I asked her if she would. I felt a little nervous about asking and Joan offered to help me through this."

"That serious is it?"

Helen didn't reply but just shook her head.

"Right then let's be hearing what it is that is so personal Helen."

Helen again coughed to clear her throat. She glanced across at Joan seeking the encouragement to start talking.

"Well I was wondering if you could tell me about where I came from, Mrs. Freeman."

Mrs. Freeman's face showed signs of surprise. Of all the things that she had been thinking this was not one of them.

"What do you mean Helen?"

"I know that I came here in 2000 from my foster parents in Dodworth near Barnsley. I know that I stayed with them from the age of eight and that I had to leave because Mrs. James lost her husband and she became ill. I was very sad to leave I was so happy there."

"Why are you not happy here then Helen?"

"Oh yes Mrs. Freeman but…

"I am glad to hear that Helen. I have to say that I was not expecting this sort of conversation when you told me that it was a personal thing that you had to discuss. I am sorry but it would not be lawful if I discussed this in front of Joan here even though you feel the need to have her here. I therefore will have to ask her to leave us if this conversation carries on. This is up to you Helen as I say I am not allowed to discuss this with anyone other than you. In fact some years ago I would not have been able to discuss it with you."

Helen looked again at Joan. Joan mouthed that she would leave and see her later.

"Thank you Joan I will be all right now I think."

Joan left the room wondering what Helen was about to discover about her background if anything.

Mrs. Freeman walked over to some filing cabinets that stood along one of the walls. Each had labels indication whatever was in there alphabetically. Helen watched, as Mrs. Freeman seemed to go into one of the filing cabinets labelled E – G and withdrew a fairly thick file from within the drawer. Mrs. Freeman sat down at her desk and browsed through the file that lay in front of her. She never spoke for what seemed to Helen like a lifetime. Then she looked up from the file and gazed into the eyes of Helen.

"I see that you had a number of foster parents Helen. How many can you remember?"

Helen thought for a moment before she answered.

"I say I can remember Mr. and Mrs. James at Dodworth. Before those two I stayed with Mrs Hackforth but that was a short stay she already had two sons and two more foster children staying with her. I believe that she lived at a place called Darton. I think that I was either six or seven when I stayed there. I can remember changing schools but I was never there long enough to make friends I was so unhappy. That was why I felt happier when I stayed at Mrs. James's but friends were never easy. That was why Joan, she is my first true friend." Helen tried to control the tears that were building up behind her eyes. Mrs. Freeman saw this and offered her a paper handkerchief.

"I understand Helen just calm yourself we don't want you upset do we?"

"No Mrs. Freeman. I am sorry."

"Go on then Helen what else do you remember about your past?"

Helen thought trying to place things in the correct order in her mind.

"I remember a Mr. and Mrs. Taylor I thought that they were my parents because I seemed to be with them for so long."

"Do you remember where they lived?"

"I remember going to a school at a place I think they called Birdwell. I think I can remember the house where I lived. It was rather small but there were no children. I always wanted a brother and a sister but they never had any. I cannot ever remember thinking that I would leave them one day. Then I was told by somebody that came to the house that I was to move to live with someone else."

"How did you feel about that then Helen?"

Again tears flooded but this time Helen could not control them. Mrs. Freeman came around the desk and placed her arms around her shoulders to comfort her.

"There, there come on don't get yourself so upset otherwise we will have to stop this conversation. I can't have you getting yourself so upset."

"Sorry Mrs. Freeman I promised myself that I would not become upset by this. I feel that there is a gap in my life. I feel that I have bits and pieces and I do not feel whole."

Mrs. Freeman could see that this was so important to Helen and had already made her mind up to help her as much as the law would allow her.

"Do you know what happened to Mrs. James then did she ever keep in contact with you?"

"No I wrote her a letter just after I was taken from there but I got no reply. I don't know if she is still ill."

Helen hesitated. "She could have died, oh I hope she didn't that would be awful."

"No Helen she didn't die but she is still very ill. I could arrange for you to go and see her if you thought that would help."

Helen lifted her eyes from down her chest.

"Do you think that she would see me? I would be very nervous, but it would be nice."

"I will see what I can arrange I have no idea when or if they will allow her to have visitors. Tell me do you know if they had any other family?"

Helen thought for a moment.

"Do you know I believe I did hear them talk about a son but throughout all the years I lived there I never actually saw him I really don't know; sorry I can't be more helpful."

"Right then will you leave that with me. I will then seek out what is possible for you and I will call you back when I have more information for you."

"Could I have a look at my file Mrs. Freeman?"

A very embarrassed smile appeared over the face of Mrs. Freeman.

"I am so sorry Helen but I am not allowed to. I know it seems strange but the law won't allow me to show you what is written… I know what you are thinking and I have to agree with you, but the law is the law."

Mrs. Freeman stood up from behind her desk. "Right then I will contact you when I have some news Helen. I believe that you have a class now so if you feel all right then I would go along to it."

Helen thanked her and inside she did feel a lot better now that there appeared to be something-positive happening even though she had not leaned a great deal.

Helen made her way along the corridor towards the lecture room. Joan was stood outside waiting for her. Her face was full of anticipation as she waited for any news that Helen may have to tell her.

"What happened in there Helen?"

"Nothing much but I do feel that the meeting has given me some hope of finding more about my background. Apparently laws that do not allow me to read about what is in my records but Mrs.

Freeman did agree to help me as much as she can. She was very nice about it and in fact she is trying to get permission for me to visit Mrs. James in hospital.

"Was she your last foster parent then?"

"Yes her husband died and although I knew that she was ill I had no idea what happened after that."

Joan squeezed Helen's hand.

"Well we can only hope that she can help Helen. Whatever I will be by your side throughout if you want me."

Helen smiled and that said it all.

"I would like that Joan and thank you I don't think that I would have gone this far if it had not been for you."

Chapter Three.

The next three weeks went by and there had been no contact from anyone apart from other Homelands business by Mrs. Freeman.
Then one day, it was a Tuesday morning Mrs. Freeman sent for Helen to attend her office.
Helen felt very nervous even though she had wanted this day to come a great deal quicker than it had. She quickly called and told Joan that she was going to see Mrs. Freeman. Joan wished her good luck and reminded her of her offer to be by her side.
Helen knocked on the office door and instantly got a response from Mrs. Freeman.
"Come in Helen I have some good news for you. Mrs. James is in Barnsley in the hospital there and she is allowed visitors. They have told her about your wish to see her and she has agreed to see you. I must tell you not to expect too much though she is

still very ill. In fact they are about to move her to a local hospice in the next few weeks."

Helen felt a mixture of feelings, happiness that Mrs. James had agreed to see her but sadness that she was still very ill.

"When do you think you will go over to see her Helen? I have agreed that I would give the hospital a day or so notice."

"I would like to go as soon as is possible."

"Right then I will make the necessary arrangements. Will you be going alone or will you be taking Miss Fields?"

"Yes I would like Joan to come with me. I would feel safer if I had someone with me. I know that it is not far but…

"It's all right Helen I understand you can't be too careful these days."

The arrangements were made and Helen and Joan caught the bus that would take them to Barnsley. A short ride in a taxi from the bus station saw them stood outside the hospital.

"How do you feel Helen?"

"Fine Joan, I feel fine. Mrs. James was a lovely person and I was so happy there. She was a lot of fun when her husband was alive. They had so many hobbies; her husband I know liked the horses...

"They had horses?"

"Oh no he liked the horse racing he used to get very excited when they were on the television. They used to take me for lovely walks and they knew all the birds and the Latin names that they were called. I loved living there even though I called her mum I knew that she was not really my mum but it felt right. You know what I mean, don't you Joan?"

"I think so but I was never really… well you know what I mean?"

"Yes I think so. Anyway let's go in and see her. They may only allow me at her bedside but you won't mind waiting for me will you?"

"Not at all, she is your mum I am just pleased to be here with you."

"Thanks Joan. You are a true friend."

They walked into the large entrance of the hospital and called at the reception desk to enquire which ward Mrs. James was on. The young person behind the reception desk looked at the computer and told them and showed them where the lift was that would take them up to the correct floor.

They arrived on the eighth floor and approached the nurse's desk and asked about Mrs. James. She looked at Helen and Joan and asked if they were relatives. Helen explained that she was fostered by Mrs. James but had lost contact. She explained how Mrs. Freeman had made arrangements that would enable her to visit her. The nurse looked in a book that sat on the desk.

"Ah yes it is in here but it just says the visit would be by a Miss Helen Taylor, but no one else."

"Oh this is my friend Joan I would like her to come with me but if it is a problem she will stay here if that is all right."

The nurse studied both the girls for a moment.

"Yes I suppose it cannot do any harm. I didn't think that Mrs. James had any family in fact she has not had many visitors all the time that she has been in here. It is such a pity that peoples like her have so few friends. I understand she has done so much for so many people and children. It is such a pity."

Helen felt sharpness in the nurse's voice. And felt that she had to explain her situation.

"I did write to her almost a year ago but got no reply and I could not get over here to visit. I didn't even know she was in here until a few days ago. I did think that she had a son but I have never seen him."

"Well he has not been here to see her so he should be ashamed of himself if he does exist."

"Can we go in then?"

The nurse nodded and told them that they should not worry if she seems to be asleep. "Just talk to her and she may open her eyes."

Helen walked into the small side ward in front of Joan. There were four other beds all with aged people lying in them. It looked a sorry sight, as they all seemed to just lie there helpless.

Helen looked around the beds and at first could not see Mrs. James. Then she spotted a frail looking lady lying with her eyes closed just beside the window that overlooked the town of Barnsley. Helen felt the tears bubble up inside at the sight of this old looking lady that was once so lively and happy. Now she lay here on this bed helpless and so sad looking. This was not the mum that she had known. She stopped and stood gazing for a few moments building up her feelings as not to show Mrs. James her sadness.

Helen finally approached the bed and immediately took hold of the lady's hand and gave it a loving squeeze. There was no reaction at first but then her eyes slowly opened up and looked at the person holding her hand. She managed a small smile but it only showed across her lips but her eyes were still holding that sad look.

Helen had no idea if Mrs. James had recognised her so she gave her time to come around and then told her who she was.

The eyes told everything she had no idea who Helen was, but Helen still held on to her hand. Mrs. James moved her eyes without actually moving her head to look at the second person who was stood over her bed. She still managed that smile though and Helen knew that this was the reaction of someone who cared inside about all people.

Kindness was a part that illness could never destroy.

Helen carried on talking telling Mrs. James that this was her friend Joan and talked about things that they used to do together. She talked about Mr. James and his horse racing and the bird watching. Mrs. James looked at Helen all the time that she was talking and offered a smile every now and then as though she was recognising what Helen was telling her.

Helen knew that she didn't know but it seemed such a natural thing to do. Why should they not talk about those days that had given them all such happiness?

Then from nowhere came a song into her mind and Helen started to sing it quietly. 'Moon River' Helen hummed through the words. She had sung this song on many occasions at the James's home. Mrs. James said that it was their song from many years previous and meant such a lot to both of them.

Helen was sure that some brightness came into those sad eyes and she wondered whether or not the tune had registered with Mrs. James.

Helen and Joan stayed for over one hour until the nurse came along and told them that they should leave in case they were tiring Mrs. James out. Helen tried to take her hand from Mrs. James's but suddenly the hand took hold and it was obvious that she wanted to hold on to this young lady that seemed to know so much about her.

"I think she knows who I am. Look she is holding my hand like a parent would when the child wanted to move away."

The nurse shook her head. "I am sorry love but it does not mean anything she just feels your hand and likes to hold on to it. It could me mine it would not change anything."

"No I know she recognises me. I will come again soon; you will see she will recognise me."

Helen took one look back as they left the ward but Mrs. James had fallen into a sleep once more, back to the routine of the day in that ward.

Tears rolled down her face has they left the hospital and Joan allowed the tears top fall freely she knew that it would do more harm than good to stop her from grieving at that moment.

When they arrived back at Homelands Mrs. Freeman asked Helen to go and see her in her office. Helen arrived and was amazed at the way in which Mrs. Freeman treated her. Normally she was a lady that although not over strict but someone that you always felt would not allow you to get too near.

"Would care for a cup of tea Helen?"

"Yes lease Mrs. Freeman that would be lovely."

"Right then tell me how you got on at the hospital. Did Mrs. James.. How was she?"

"She looked very sad and pitiful, not the lady that I knew, not the mum that she was. It was so sad her eyes had lost the brightness and the life that was once there no this was not the person that I knew, not at first."

Mrs. James looked surprised at the last statement. "How do you mean Helen, not at first?"

"Well I spoke to her about the many things that we had all done together over those years, those happy days we had spent together. I held her hand and we looked each other in the eye but I didn't see any recognition there in those sad eyes. Then I remembered a song that we sung many times and I knew that it was a favourite of Mr and Mrs. James's. 'Moon River' I can't remember who sand it but I think he was an American…

"Andy Williams, that was who sang it. It was one of my favourites too. I still have the record in my collection."

"That's right that's the name. They both loved it I think it had some importance in their marriage but I don't know what."

"Yes a lot of people have songs that are significant in their relationships. I… no it doesn't matter I am being childish."

Silence as both of them suddenly had their own thoughts about the past.

"Will you visit the hospital again Helen?"

"Yes I can't allow her just to disappear from my life. I intend going as often as I can before they transfer her to that hospice. No I know that she recognised me never mind what that nurse thinks."

"I am pleased about that Helen. If it would help I could allow you to take my record along with you. Perhaps the hospital would allow you to play it to her for a short while."

"Thank you Mrs. Freeman. Thank you for your offer it may help I do hope so if I could….

"Do not get your hopes up too much Helen. You know that she has been ill for some time and they would not transfer to the hospice if they thought that she could get better."

Helen went along most weekends to see Mrs. James then it was about four weeks into her weekend visits that something happened. She arrived at the hospital as per usual and took the lift to the ward. Helen walked into the ward but when she looked for Mrs. James she was gone. Helen's heart pounded inside the fear built she wanted to scream out.

She turned and headed for the nurse's desk where the nurse was on duty that first met her of the very first visit.

"Where is Mrs. James?"

"Gone, she's gone. They took her yesterday but you knew that she was going."

"Gone where?"

"To the hospice yes she went to the hospice yesterday."

"Where is the hospice?"

"Not far in fact it is in the grounds of the hospital so you have not far to go."

"Thank you and thank you for taking care of her while she was here."

"That's fine it is my job. By the way a man came to see her two days ago."

"A man, who was he?"

"He told us that he was her son. He had just arrived from Australia. Apparently he moved there many years ago."

"How old was he?"

"Oh I don't know if I was taking a guess I'd say around thirty or there- about. He's very handsome if I wasn't married I think that I could fancy him."

They both laughed and the tension that Helen had felt towards the nurse disappeared.

"Thank you again."

"I do hope that you find what you are looking for."

"I will I am sure of that."

Helen arrived at the hospice and introduced herself to the staff. Mrs. James was in a side room and the first thing that Helen asked the nurse was if it would be all right to play the Andy Williams record to Mrs. James.

They agreed it was obviously a very different atmosphere to that within the hospital. The first priority here was the comfort of the patient as in the hospital, yes it was comfort but they had too much to do and too little time to do it in.

Helen played Moon River over and over again to Mrs. James. The sadness in those eyes began slowly to disappear and there was a sign of the brightness that Helen knew when they all lived together. Helen carried on with the same routine over the three weeks on her visits. She would talk about the past and what she remembered about Mr. James. She didn't know whether or not Mrs. James had any idea as to what she was on about but it made no difference to Helen. In fact Helen was sure that she did understand and even the staff there remarked about the difference that noticed since Mrs. James first arrived. After this time suddenly

Helen saw a significant change in Mrs. James. When Helen arrived at the hospice the first thing that Mrs. James did was to take hold of her hand and give it a squeeze.

Helen felt really good inside was her patience making a difference. She could only hope she knew that Mrs. James would not want to die if she returned to the Mrs. James that Helen once knew. The changes became more apparent and Helen was shocked when on one of her visits Mrs. James was sat up in bed. Helen just stood at the door of the ward and looked in amazement at what was there before her eyes.

She rushed forward and took hold of Mrs. James and gave her a big hug. Mrs. James smiled but it was not the smile of someone who had recognised someone who had been lost.

"Hello there you are the nice person that has been visiting me aren't you?"

Tears flooded into Helen's eyes as she realised that Mrs. James had not recognised her as the Helen who she looked after for all those years.

"Yes Mrs. James I am and I have to say that you look a lot better today."

"I feel much better thank you. Are you a nurse then? I once wanted to be a nurse you know."

"No Mrs. James I am just a friend."

For a slight moment the smile left Mrs. James's face.

"A friend you say. I am so sorry I don't believe that I know you, do I?"

"It doesn't matter we became friends whilst you were in here. I came to visit you when you were really sick."

"Oh that was very nice of you. Have I been sick then? I was wondering why I was here this is not my home. I was thinking that I had to get my husband's dinner ready but the nurse told me that it had been taken care of and that I should concentrate on getting better."

"Yes that is right you have always worked hard and now it is your turn to be pampered for a while."

Mrs. James gave Helen's hand another squeeze.

"What is your name dear?"

"It is Helen, I am called Helen Taylor."

"Hello Helen Taylor do you think that we could listen to that record, you know 'Moon River'. It is my favourite you know. My husband and I dance to that every time we hear it."

"Yes I am sure that we can. I will just place it on for you."

Helen turned her eyes flooding with tears but she didn't want to show Mrs. James that she was so upset. She knew that there would be no way that she could explain her feelings perhaps one day, hopefully one day soon.

The record started and Mrs. James closed her eyes and let the sound take hold of her mind and body. Helen just looked down at this still frail looking lady as the enjoyment of what she was hearing flooded her mind away from her illness.

After the song finished Mrs. James slowly opened her eyes and smiled.

"Will Eddy be coming soon Helen?"

"Eddy?"

"Yes my husband silly. Will he be coming to see me I want him to here Moon River. He will be amazed that they have it here. Fancy the hospital having our tune here it is amazing."

"I don't know whether he will be coming today. I can enquire if you like I will go and talk to one of the nurses she may know."

Helen knew that she had to remove herself from there just for a moment. Her inside was awash with emotion and she knew that anytime it would break out and that would be so upsetting for Mrs. James.

"I will be back in a moment. Shall I put the music back on for you until I return?"

"If you would my love, it would be so nice."

Helen walked swiftly out of the room and along the corridor towards the nurse station. She was wiping the tears away as they ran down her cheeks. A young nurse came over to her and asked if she could help. Helen had met her before on one of her visits so the nurse knew whom Helen had been to see.

"Mrs. James seems a lot more cheerful these days Helen. I can call you Helen can't I?"

"Yes that's all right. Yes, she does seem a great deal brighter. What do the doctors think?"

"I don't really know they don't tell us much. All that I can say is that her functions are what we would call normal. She is still having problems with her mind though."

"Yes I had noticed that. Would you think that this could improve, you know."

"I can't tell you that. She is an unusual case though not one we normally have in here. We, the nurses that is, have been remarking that Mrs. James does not look like a terminal case to us. We are having great difficulty in understanding why it is that she was placed in here. Have you any idea as to the reason Helen?"

Helen shook her head. "I didn't even know that she was in hospital until a few months ago. You see Mr. and Mrs. James fostered me when I was eight and I lived with them until I was sixteen."

"Oh so you know them well then. How was it that you say you had never known that she was ill until a few months ago t

Helen found this question hard to answer. She had already asked herself that question over and over again. She could not find an answer that would satisfy her never mind some caring outsider.

"If I could answer that question I would but you see I thought that they had abandoned me and didn't want to know me anymore. Silly after all those years but that is what I thought."

"Why did they do that then?"

"I just don't know me, we were so happy and then suddenly Mr. James died and Mrs. James seemed to give up and could not manage to look after me."
"How did Mr. James die then had he been ill for some time?"
"No not at all. We had been bird watching on the moors and the day had been brilliant. We had a picnic and we lay in the grass with our binoculars looking out for rare birds. Mr. and Mrs. James became very excited at some bird that was hovering over the moor. I believe they said it was some sort of eagle but I don't know.
They talked about it all the way home and we had a lovely meal and I went to my room and did some homework. It was one of the reasons that we had gone out there because of my homework. I had to write an essay about English wildlife and Mr. and Mrs. James were always keen that I did well.
Anyway I must have fallen to sleep when I heard such a rumpus downstairs. I ran down and Mr

James was on the floor and Mrs. James was crying, well screaming over him. I rang for help and the paramedics came but it was too late. He had suffered a heart attack and just died.
I was so shocked I didn't know what I should do. Mrs. James was hysterical and I could do nothing. I remember thinking why can't I cry. Anyway they took him away and Mrs. James was ill in bed and I had to try and look after her and myself and go to school. These people came along and the next thing I knew I was in this place called Homelands."
"What a shock for you it was remarkable that you weren't ill after all that."
"I know but that is why I never made contact with her I was afraid that she may reject me and I don't think that I could have taken that."
"I don't think that I could have neither you poor girl."
The nurse had placed a hand on Helen's shoulder to try and comfort her. Helen had always

wondered why people did this but it did seem to work.

They both turned as they heard footsteps coming along the corridor.

"How about this one Helen he looks a bit of all right then?"

Down the corridor walking towards them was a tanned young man smartly dressed wearing what was unusual these days, a suit and a tie he watched his every step and he was suddenly aware that his every movement was being scrutinised by these two young ladies along the corridor.

"Good morning."

"Good morning, that is not an English accent, where are you from?"

"Australia nurse, but originally from here. Yes I am a local boy believe it or believe it not."

Helen remembered what the nurse had told her at the hospital about a young man from Australia. Could this be Mrs. James's son?"

"Local boy from Australia that sounds interesting. What brings you back here then?"

"Well nurse I am here to see my mother."

"Mother we have no Australian mothers here, not that I know of anyway."

"I didn't say that she was Australian nurse."

Helen started to interrupt. "Tell me is Mrs. James your mother?"

"That's right love my name is Andrew but who are you. You don't work here do you?"

"No I don't. I am here visiting your mother also."

"You know my mother?"

"Yes I know her very well. I was her…."

"How is she? Any better than the last time I came. She didn't know who I was then. I hope you people have been able to help her. Sorry love you were saying?"

"Nothing it is not important."

"Alright then can I go and see her?"

The nurse looked at Helen and saw Helen give her the nod.

"Yes just go down the corridor and your mother is in room ten. Take care not to upset her whilst you are in there. If she still doesn't recognise you don't go pushing her. We don't want you spoiling any good work that we have achieved."

"Hold on love I am not here to fight my mother I just want to make sure that she is all right."

The young man left them and the nurse was obviously not well pleased with the arrogant way in which this young man had talked to her.

"He maybe handsome Helen but his manners are not too good. Why didn't you tell him who you were?"

"It is not important. The important thing is that he does not upset her and maybe they can rekindle the relationship that they once had. They don't need me for that."

"What nonsense you talk Helen. He should be grateful to you for what you have achieved. I know our doctors are."

"The doctors, why what have they been saying about me?"

"Oh nothing it was just something I overheard, that's all."

"Come on you can't leave me like that. What have they been saying?"

"Well I overheard them saying that you appeared to be doing more good than all the medicines that they were prescribing. They agreed that they should take out some of them and give you time to work your miracles. There, but don't you dare let them know that I have told you."

Helen felt quite jubilant inside and it helped to overcome some of the sadness she had been feeling when she left the room when Mrs. James asked who she was.

"Listen I won't say anything. I don't even know your name, what is it?"

"Jill, Jill Greaves."

"I am Helen Taylor Jill and I am so pleased to have met you."

They both laughed as they realised that somewhere in there was some sort of understanding between them.

"I think I will leave him to talk with his mother Jill I will come back tomorrow. If Mrs. James asks about me tell her I will be back tomorrow. I would feel uncomfortable if I went in whilst he was in there."

"I can understand that Helen. Anyway he should spend time with his mother I think he has a right cheek. I will be on duty tomorrow from ten in the morning till ten at night."

"I don't know how you can do all those hours I don't think that I could and I am younger than you."

"You do get used to it and the money helps you know. I have two kids to take care of and they don't come cheap. I had to buy my eldest some school shoes the other week you will never guess how much I had to pay Helen."

Helen shook her head she knew that she had trouble when it came to money matters and she had only herself to consider.

"How much were they then Jill?"

"Thirty pounds and he was not happy about that. The kids set each other off you know. They all want designer gear and they are just not practical not for school. They cost about seventy pounds and I bet they would not last two months not with my lad."

"What does your husband do?"

"Not a lot he left us some three years ago. I have no idea where he is and what is more I don't want to know the kids keep asking me but they didn't see what I had to put up with. Boozing, gambling and I suspected he was seeing someone else on the side. I kept finding little things that made me suspicious."

"That must have been terrible Jill. Did he hit you then?"

"He tried but I hit him with the frying pan that stopped him in his tracks. He was only like that when he had drunk too much. The number of times he came home drunk was on the increase and I didn't, no I was not willing to put up with that. Besides I was past caring for him anymore. We had to get married and I think that I was too young but you think that you know everything. Mother warned me but I simply ignored her like kids do. You must have…. sorry Helen me and my big mouth."

"It's all right Jill I do understand what you are talking about."

Helen left the hospice and she tried to get her mind around the things that had happened that morning.

Firstly there was the meeting with Andrew James and the arrogance of the man. Then she wondered about Jill's children and how she had said that they missed their father. She knew what that felt like and wondered if they wished that they could just have a normal father that showed love and kindness.

Helen arrived back at Homelands and saw Joan walking in the grounds. She waved and Joan walked over towards her.

"Helen and how did you find Mrs. James today any more improvement?"

"She seems to be getting a lot brighter I don't know about after today though"

"Why what happened today?"

"Her son turned up at the hospice such an arrogant person."

"Her son but I didn't know that she had a son."

"Well no, I didn't until the nurse at the hospital told me that some man had been to see her and that he had come all the way from Australia."

"Had he? Come from Australia then."

"Oh yes he was tanned and some would say very handsome."

"Handsome how old was he?"

"You are not thinking of….

"Well why not I am available if he is. Did he mention whether or not he had a wife tucked away somewhere?"

"I am sorry Joan I never got around to asking him that. In fact he doesn't know that his mother fostered me. I tried to tell him but he wasn't listening so I let it go."

"How do you think that his mother would take his sudden appearance?"

"I don't know I only hope that he doesn't undo all that we have achieved. The doctors apparently have been talking about me and how I have changed the outlook for Mrs. James."

"When are you going next then Helen? I wouldn't mind going with you if that would be all right?"

Helen laughed. "You Joan I know what you are being attracted by but you are always welcome. If it had not been for you I would not be in the position that I am. I would still be a lonely girl who had no idea as to where she belonged. I will always be grateful to you for that."

Mrs. James sent for Helen during Thursday afternoon. Helen thought that it may be more news on the other foster parents and felt a tinge of excitement as she made her way to the office.

Mrs. Freeman welcomed her with a heart-warming smile.

"Hello Helen, or should I be offering you my congratulations?"

Helen looked a little confused.

"Sorry Mrs. Freeman I…

"Don't be modest I have had the hospice on to me asking about you. They told me how you had helped Mrs. James and that they were now sure that whatever it was that had taken Mrs. James down until death was inevitable has now disappeared. They were asking me if you had been involved in nursing or anything that could have helped you to understand Mrs. James's problems."
"What did you say to them?"
"Just that you were a very caring and loving person and that you have this ability to make people feel better by just being there."
Helen shook her head in astonishment at what she had just been told. The doctors had never spoken to her all the time that she had been visiting Mrs. James. If Jill hadn't said that she had overheard them talking she would never have guessed.
"Thank you Mrs. Freeman. I haven't done anything really. I just talked and played that music to her and she gradually started to look a great deal

better. However she hasn't recognised me as yet and that is what I want more than anything."

"Yes I can understand that Helen. I think that you should keep going who knows the mind is a wonderful thing and it can heal itself."

"Yes I intend doing that and I would like to thank you for making all this possible. Have you any news on my other foster parents?"

"Yes and no. I have been trying to find the Hackforth's but the last address we had was Darton but they have moved. The social services are looking through their files but apparently she doesn't foster anymore so they haven't been in touch for about two years. They think that one of the sons has been in trouble with the police. They didn't say much but I felt that drugs had been involved."

"Oh that is such a shame. She must have been devastated she seemed to love all her children. In fact that was probably why she fostered children."

"Yes drugs are becoming a real problem for everyone. The parents today have a great deal to look out for. I wonder sometimes why we bother to have children but then none of us would be here would we?"

"No but then some of us don't know our parents and I think that this is just as bad."

"Yes you are right Helen. I remember my mother telling me how she felt when my grandfather was killed in the Second World War. I never met him of course but I did spend a lot of time with my grandmother and she showed me photographs of them when they were married. After all those years she still loved him and she never re-married. My mother would tell me how he used to tell them stories about all sorts of things. There were no televisions then and the family was always important it is those times that goes to show me how things have changed. Families break away and not only do they lose something it also says things about communities. They were once like families and then things changed and I am sure that we all lost something when that happened."

Helen felt the sadness in the voice of Mrs. Freeman. She thought that there was a sad story there somewhere.

"Her son turned up the other day Mrs. Freeman."

"What Mrs. James's son? I didn't know she had one."

"Apparently she had he lives in Australia and has done for a number of years now. Well I met him on Tuesday and Jill and me…."

"Jill don't you mean Joan?"

"No Jill is the nurse who looks after Mrs. James. She is lovely and she has problems too. She kicked her husband out. He drank and hit her and carried on with other women. There are two children involved and according to her they miss their father."

"Yes there always are children involved and they feel the breakdown the worst they don't understand grown-ups and their problems do they?"

"I don't suppose that they do. I don't understand any of the grown-ups that have been in my life but I am trying to. "

"Sorry again Helen I do seem to keep putting my foot in it don't I feel that I have known you for so long since you came to see me what was it, four months ago?"

"It must be but it only seems like yesterday. Anyway I won't keep you any longer and thank you once again for your help."

Mrs. Freeman smiled but inside the conversation had reminded her of her own childhood and things that had happened to her.

She sat down and placed her hands on to her head. Tears filled her eyes as she thought of her father and how he had become ill and her mother changed because she thought that he would not pull through. They had found a prostate cancer and they had heard how serious this was and how many people especially men died from it.

She remembered how well he was and the shock that he had to go into hospital after a visit to the doctors took them all by surprise.

She remembered how she tried to comfort her mother and inside she was wondering what she would do if she had no father. How could he leave me when I was only sixteen years of age? Who could I talk to about it? There was no one I tried my grandmother but she tried but it didn't help. She had lost her husband when they were so young but didn't know what it felt to lose a father. My mother must know how I feel but she is too wrapped up in her own loss or the danger of it.

After three months things turned around and we became much more of a family they had caught the cancer early and that had saved my father's life. I had prayed to God to not take my daddy away from me and he had helped me.

Mrs. Freeman took her hands away from her head and looked down at the photograph that stood on her desk. She picked it up and kissed the two people on it.

She felt more determined that she would help Helen find the thing that she was missing most and knew then that Helen's life could never be complete if she didn't help her.

Chapter Four

Joan went along to the hospice with Helen on the following Saturday. Helen still was not clear as to the real reason for her company but she didn't mind. Joan had helped her and the fact that she was curious about the mysterious son was only natural. From what she had learned about Joan since they met was that she was a bit of a flirt if given the opportunity and they had often laughed about it. Arriving at the hospice around eleven o'clock Helen met Jill. "Good morning Jill I don't believe that you have met my friend Joan. Joan Fields this is Jill Greaves she is doing a fine job looking after Mrs. James. Over worked and under paid and terrible hours as usual."

Jill laughed. "Yes you could say that but I am happy that is the main thing."

"Well that means a lot these days. There are so many things outside that seem to make life difficult for a lot of people."

"That is so true Joan but some of which is brought on people themselves wanting more than they can afford. I do not have that luxury."

"No and I do not Jill."

"Has the arrogant son been this morning Jill?"

"No not yet. Actually he was quite charming when he left yesterday. In fact he asked me about you Helen."

Helen felt herself start to blush.

"Asking about me was he? What did he want then?"

"He was praising your efforts with his mother apparently one of the doctors told him how hard you had been working with his mother."

Oh yes apparently they rang our Mrs. Freeman about it. I wish that they would not make such a fuss about it. I want to do it like any other daughter would."

"Helen but you are not her daughter so don't put your efforts down."

"Jill is right; I keep telling you that you are something special Helen. Don't I?"

"Yes you do but I don't think that I am."

"Well the improvement continues Helen Mrs. James was asking for you this morning."

"You mean she has remembered who I am?"

Jill's expression told it all. "No not that Helen, I am sorry. No she wanted to know where that lovely girl was who played her music to her and talked to her about interesting things."

"Oh I see well that is an improvement certainly from some weeks ago. She had no idea what I was doing then. Never mind the main thing is that she is showing positive signs."

Helen and Joan walked towards the room where Mrs. James was staying.

The expression on Mrs. James's face said it better than a thousand words when Helen walked into the room. Helen walked immediately to her bedside and took hold of the outstretched hand of Mrs. James's.

The smile turned Helen's and Joan insides into water. It was the first time that Joan had seen Mrs. James since that first week that she and Helen went to the hospital. Joan was only in the ward for a few minutes but that was the picture she had in her mind. The sight of a very old lady searching for the end to take her away from the misery that she was feeling then. This was not that same woman that half sat up in her bed. The eyes were bright and the smile stretched the old looking wrinkles from her face.

She did not have the same relationship with this woman but still tears filled her eyes.

Helen introduced Joan to Mrs. James and she smiled showing that she was welcome and that she was pleased that she was there.

Helen talked about the man and that she knew that he was her son. The face of Mrs. James crinkled up showing that she was pleased that they had met. She tried to mouth to Helen how pleased she was that he had come to see her.

Helen told her that he would be back to see her perhaps later that day. She also said that it was a pity that he hadn't managed to come home to see his father.

Immediately the expression on Mrs. James face changed and she shook her head. Helen saw that this had upset Mrs. James and turned the conversation away from it by talking about the days when they went out bird watching.

They talked again for another hour and Joan excused herself to go to the toilet. In fact she just wanted to leave Helen alone with Mrs. James for a moment.

She walked along the corridor and saw this tanned young man walking towards her. Her heart jumped a beat as she realised that this had to be Mrs. James's son.

He came along side her and from nowhere she found the courage to speak to him.

"Hello you don't know me but are you Andrew James?"

The man looked shocked he was not expecting this from this lovely looking girl.

"Yes do I know you? I am sorry if I do but I was thinking of something else at the time."

"That is all right no you don't know me. I am a good friend of Helen Taylor. We have been visiting your mother."

"Oh yes I can't thank you enough for what you have been doing to help her. I must meet both of you away from the hospice so that we can talk about the past years."

"That would be nice perhaps we could have a drink together."

"Yes that would be good we must arrange it sometime."

"Well I am free tonight if you are."

Andrew looked shocked even for him this straight talking was not expected. He was not used to girls taking the lead when it came to this sort of thing.

"Well it would be nice but I can't not tonight I am meeting a school friend. He rang me the other day when he realised that I was back in England."

"Sorry I just thought…."

"No, no that is all right how about tomorrow night. We could meet up at the Coach and Horses just down the road from here. Do you know it?"

"Yes that will be fine tomorrow then about eight o'clock."

"Right then I must go I need to talk to mother about something."

Andrew smiled and carried on along the corridor. Joan moved towards where Jill was working at the nurse's desk.

"You look excited Joan."

"Yes I am I have just got a date with that man from Australia."

"What Andrew James?"

"Yes isn't he divine?"

"Well I wouldn't know but you have been quick. What did Helen say?"

"She doesn't know as yet."

Jill laughed you young girls you don't hand about do you?"

"No life is too short."

Andrew walked into his mother's room and Helen sat with her back to the door and jumped when he spoke she thought that it was Joan returning.

"You must be the Florence Nightingale that they all keep telling me about. We met the other day didn't we?"

"Yes but my name is Helen and I am no Florence Nightingale. I am here because I care. Why are you here?"

Andrew suddenly realised that he had overstepped the mark.

"Sorry I didn't mean to….

"No I am sure that you didn't. Perhaps we should introduce ourselves properly if only for your mother's sake."

"Yes I agree."

"I am Andrew and I have been living in Australia for over ten years. A friend wrote to me and told me that my mother was ill. I was out in the bush so it was almost twelve months before I received the letter."

Helen shook her head suggesting that she understood but inside she could not come to terms with the fact that he had left them all those years ago.

"What about you how do you know my mother?"

"She was my foster mother."

Andrew's face took on a look of surprise. He didn't even know that his mother and father even wanted to foster children.

"How long did you stay with her, them?"

"I was eight years of age when they took me in and I moved away when I was sixteen. I didn't understand then but I can see why now. I thought that they didn't like me no more but that was not true."

"What happened then that you had to leave?"

"It was after your father died it was very sad and I didn't know how to cope with it. Your mother held me together but inside she had died but never let it be shown. She knew that she had to find me a good home because she thought that…."

Helen stopped as the tears flowed freely down her face. Mrs. James face changed and she screwed her face and tears ran down her cheeks.

What was this man doing to this kind young girl that had showed her great kindness? Her hand took a stronger hold of Helen's hand.

Helen looked at her and assured her that she was all right. Andrew stood up and placed his arms around her. Helen felt uncomfortable by this. He may be Mrs. James's son but he was a stranger to her and she moved away from the enclosed arm.

"I am sorry to open old wounds Helen."

"It's all right it is not your fault. I thought that I had dealt with it a long time ago but I obviously have been fooling myself. Anyway I am all right now. No your mother found me this place at Homelands in Doncaster. I didn't think about her feelings in all of this just that once again I had been taken away from a place that I loved and people that I loved."

"Yes I can understand that. I have felt like that for many years myself. The thought that I could be rejected by someone who I loved very much and who I thought loved me in the same way."

Helen thought that Andrew was talking about a girlfriend that had deserted him at some time but never asked.

The conversation came around to the family and how Helen went bird watching with Andrew's mother and father and how they walked through the countryside and laughed at so many things. Life was so good for all of those years and then suddenly it changed. I blamed God I blamed everything and everybody. I was not nice to know and I turned my back on our mother.

I didn't even know of your existence all the time that I lived with your parents I never ever heard them talk about you. I never ever saw any photographs of you around the house.

"I am not surprised now I suppose that I understand their feeling better now than I did then. Unfortunately we can't turn the clock back can we?"

"No life in hindsight could often be better but then we would not have learned a great deal from the many mistakes that we all make through our lives would we?"

Perhaps we can meet up and discuss the past few years. I have missed a great deal and you could perhaps help me with those missing years. I know that we are meeting for a drink tomorrow…

"Are we I didn't know that. When did we arrange that then?"

"Your friend arranged it with me earlier, Joan I think she said he name was."

"Yes that is my friend all right."

"Is it all right then?"

"I suppose so but where are we meeting?"

"In the Coach and Horses down the road if that is all right it is just for a drink but I would seriously like to meet up with just you to go over those past years. I hope that we can become friends."

"We can only try and as long as we remember that it is your mother that is important in whatever we say or do then it will be all right."

"I agree and I can assure you that is all that I want. I may not have shown my feelings to her for all these years but that would be a wrong thought. When I tell you my side of this saddening story I hope that you will see and more importantly understand."

They both said their goodbye's to Mrs. James and made their way back along the corridor. Jill was standing behind the desk have a conversation with Joan. They both looked up and smiled when they heard voices approaching them. Joan was feeling a little guilty because as yet she had not told Helen that she had made a date with Andrew. She was not too sure what Helen would make of that situation.

Joan greeted Helen a little nervously.

"Hello Helen I was just telling Jill here how much improvement I had seen in Mrs. James since I last saw her."

Helen smiled "Yes we are leased aren't we Jill?"

"Oh very pleased and what do you think Mr. James?"

"Marvellous I think that between you and Helen here it is obvious that she is feeling much better. In fact I am going to speak to the doctors to see if there is any reason as to why mother can't come home. I will be staying there for some time now so I can take care of any needs that she may have. I am sure that I can have a nurse to come in and tend her if she has any medical needs. It is no good having money if you don't use it to help yourself and the family."

Joan looked at Helen and Helen knew exactly what Joan was thinking.

"I here we are all going to the Coach and Horses tomorrow night then Joan. That was a bit of a surprise when Andrew here invited me."

"Ah yes I was going to tell you when we got back, you Andrew taking the wind out of my sails."

"I'm sorry I thought that you had intended that the invitation included Helen."

"What about me then?"

"Yes Jill you can come if you like. It is an open invitation just to welcome Andrew here back to England."

"Sorry I am here working tomorrow night but I will pop in after my shift if you are still there."

"We won't be too late as Mrs. Freeman is not one for her girls having late nights out but I think if she knows what the occasion is she will not be too critical."

"Right then see you tomorrow night. I have to go I am meeting an old pal later and once again thank you Helen I am looking forward to our discussion later."

When Andrew had gone Helen smiled at Joan.

"You crafty monkey you had no intentions of telling me about the Coach and Horses."

"Well you can't blame a girl for trying sounds like he has money too what a catch good looking and rich just what I need."

"You are disgraceful don't you think so Jill."

"Yes but what I would give for the chance."

"Anyway Helen what was that about looking forward to talking to you later?"

"Oh just that we want to talk about Mrs. James and what we both feel we should do. He didn't realise that she had fostered me for all those years. He began to think that we are like brother and sister."

"Brother and sister mm. Well that means that I have a clear road then."

"Is that all that you can think about Joan?"

"No not all of the time."

The three of them laughed not one of them would kick him out of bed but none of them were going to admit it.

"What do you think the doctors will say when he asks if Mrs. James could go home Jill?"

"I don't know but certainly the reason for bringing her here seems to have past. You know sometimes the mind plays tricks and tells the body that the body is about to die. This was what the experts saw and felt when they examined Mrs. James. The will to live had gone and there was no medicine that could cure that sort of illness. Well that spirit or devil has gone or appears to have left the body. The fact that the prodigal son has returned will do no harm either."

"That would be excellent news if it was the case. What about her memory though will that ever return to normal?"

"Who knows but ten weeks ago I would have told you if you had asked me that she would be dead by now. She was slipping that fast and we felt so helpless. That is the only problem working here that most of our patients know that they have not got long to live. It is such a shame and to see how the families rally round is such a rewarding feature. Why can't we be like that when people are healthy?"

"Right then Jill I will see you tomorrow when I come. I may be a little later than normal I am having my hair done."

"When did you arrange that then? You didn't know that we were going out."

"I arranged it a couple of weeks ago. Not all of us have to prepare are selves for a meeting with a man you know. It had nothing to do with tomorrow night. I didn't even know the man then."

"Well I suppose that I should have my hair done too can't look like something that the cat dragged in can I. Especially in front of your foster brother."

"Joan whenever have you looked like something the car dragged in I don't know a more perfect girl. You never have a hair out of place and your clothes are always smart, no jeans for you."

"Well we have to have standards Helen. Besides you are the one to talk when did you last wear a pair of jeans?"

Both of them laughed. "Don't worry Jill we are good friends really aren't we Helen?"

"Of course, but not just good friends we are best friends and hopefully we can share everything that we have."

Joan looked towards Jill.

"Now that is taking friendship a little too far. I can't say that I would be too pleased to share Andrew. I want him for myself I could eat that man he is so gorgeous."

"By you have got it bad Joan."

"When should I ask him to marry me after the first or second date, Helen what do you think Jill?"

The laughter rang down the corridor and Jill placed her fingers against her lips to suggest that they should quieten down a little.

They said their goodbyes and made their way home to Homelands.

Joan could not stop talking about Andrew and Helen was amazed at the imagination of her best friend.

Chapter Five.

Joan and Helen made their way to the Coach and Horses. They were a little early but Joan had been like a cat on hot bricks all day and Helen had to take her out to quieten her down.

"I hope that you are not going to show yourself up Joan. Take each step slowly you don't know anything about this man."

"What do I need to know he is handsome he is rich and he is adorable."

"Your head is ruling your heart Joan. We have no idea as to what he was up to in Australia he could have a wife or girlfriend out there. Who was he going to see last night he never said did he? You don't want to look as though you are desperate and then he turns you down now do you?"

Joan's face changed a little a bit of disappointment showed.

"I know that you are right Helen but I have never felt so excited about a man like I do with Andrew. Will you help me find out more and try and find if there is a girl or wife somewhere out there?"

"Of course I will but I can't just ask him like that now can I?"

"Well he may disappear from our lives."

"No I don't think so. He said that he was not going anywhere and that he would be able to take care of his mother if she was allowed out of the hospice didn't he say that?"

"That's right he did say that, didn't he? Therefore he must be planning on staying around here for a good while longer then. Perhaps he doesn't have a wife in Australia then, otherwise he would want to be there with her, wouldn't he?"

"Look Joan stop getting yourself all flustered and stop fantasising if is to happen then let happen. If there is a chance you don't want to blow it immediately now do you?"

"No you are so right Helen. I will be calm and sophisticated and play hard to get. That is my plan so there I have stopped fantasising."

Helen bought them a drink and they sat down just away from the entrance door. It was a cool night but the Coach and Horses was rather warm so the draughts from the door when people entered made it feel comfortable.

Andrew arrived straight up seven o'clock and spotted them and walked over to them. He was wearing a large grin on his face and a smart suit on his body. He looked down and saw that they both had almost full glasses of whatever it was that they were drinking.

"Can I get you another of those whilst I am at the bar girls?"

Helen shook her head. "Not for me Andrew I am all right for the moment."

"What about you then Joan can I get you one?"

"Yes please it is a gin and orange."

Andrew left them and stood at the bar waiting to be served.

"You are not on gin and orange that is just orange that I bought you."

"Well just call it Dutch courage Helen."

"Now I have seen everything you are not trying to say that you are feeling shy."

"I am absolutely petrified inside. I never ever thought that I would feel like this."

"You have got it bad Joan."

Finally Andrew joined them and placed Joan's drink down alongside her other.

"Now then girls did you go to the hospice today?"

"Helen did but I had to go to work."

"Work and what do you do?"

"I'm training to be a laboratory technician at the local college. I work three days and go to classes for the other two days and two nights."

"What is it that you wish to do then?"

I am looking to take a science course and try and get a degree. I want to, in the long term, work with those trying to stamp out cancer."

Andrew looked amazed. "That is gratifying to know. Good for you I do hope that you succeed. I understand though that they do rely on volunteers and donations to keep the research going."

"Yes that is true but there are so many people dying of this horrible thing that I am sure that it will always be funded from somewhere."

"What is it that you do then Andrew out there in the outback of Australia?"

"Something very similar to you Joan I have my degree though and I am a qualified doctor but I am currently researching those diseases that are causing the Aborigines so many problems. That is why I tend to spend a great deal of time away from civilisation hence not knowing about my family over here."

You like it then working out there. It must be very lonely all out there on your own. No company, no wife or girl friend to talk with."

Andrew didn't seem to be listening to Joan's ramblings he was too busy looking towards Helen. "No not really I have lots of company. I am not the only English person in the team. No I have two able assistants both from England who carry out the tests in the small laboratory that I have out there. Yes they are working out their own doctorates. No loneliness is something that I have noticed. Mind you after I have been home for a while that may change."

"Yes I should imagine coming back to civilisation can be a bit of a shock to the system, don't you Helen?"

Helen hesitated she didn't really want to get involved in this conversation that seemed to be going around in circles looking to see if Andrew had a wife or a girl friend.

The night passed by each trying to find out more about the other. Joan seemed to hold most of the conversation and Helen knew that this was just Joan's nerve's playing up inside her. She tried her best by changing the subject matter whenever she could. She talked about her role within the library and how they were trying to integrate student's needs to what the public wanted from a local library. It was only a part time job but this allowed her to visit Mrs. James much more than she could have if she had been in full occupation.

"You like books do you Helen?"

"Oh yes I say she does. She writes herself you know she has had several poems published."

"Is that right Helen?"

Helen blushed.

"Oh it is nothing I just dabble a little nothing too serious."

"She is also writing a novel you know. No one knows about it but she is good."

"A novel eh what's the subject then?"

Again Helen gave Joan a stern look. "It is nothing it is just fiction…

"Go on tell us about it. I am sure that Andrew would love to hear about what you think and how your mind works Helen."

"Yes Helen I would be very interested in your story."

"I am sorry but I never talk about the content it seems to stop the thought process. Remember when you are writing you are bringing things from deep inside the subconscious mind. How it got there no one can say but it is self-destruction to start trying to tell a story that at this point does not have any ending to the story. I hope that you can understand that what if someone asked you to tell them the results of something that you were investigating if at the time you had not come to any conclusions."

"I can understand that but is it going to cause all that if you just say whether it is a love story or a crime story. I don't think that would create what I think is called 'writers block' would it Helen?"

"I don't suppose so. Anyway it is both if you must know."

"I hope that you will allow me to read it when you have completed. I would love to know how your mind works. You know we do have something in common. We have both been influenced by my mother in some way or the other."

Helen decided to change the subject once more.

"Did you meet up with your friend then last night?"

"Yes we had a long chat I haven't seen him much since we left school. He was my best friend then and I suppose he would still be that today if I hadn't moved away. He's a doctor at the hospital you know. He was actually looking after my mother when she was in there. You probably met him when you were going there to see mother."

"What was his name?"

"Doctor Bellamy he is a neurologist, a good one so I am told."

"Yes I believe I did meet a doctor Bellamy. He spoke to me the first time I went there. He was not too sure as to what to make of the problems with your mother."

"Yes that is what he told me in the letter he sent to me."

Helen looked at her watch and saw that it was almost nine-thirty.

"I have to go I'm afraid. Are you coming Joan?"

Joan wanted to say no and try and make some excuse like she would wait to see if the nurse Jill Greaves made it for a drink. Then Andrew said that he had to go too so that made Joan's mind up for her.

"Yes we had better if we don't want to lose our beauty sleep. Didn't Jill say that she may call in?"

"She did but I did tell her that we may have gone by the time she finished her shift."

Andrew took hold of Helen's hand and asked her if the meeting they were to have could be sooner rather than later.

"I have found some photographs and papers that I think you would be interested in. I am staying at my mother's house in Dodworth we could meet up there. I could make us a dinner if you like."

"That would be nice. I can come over Thursday if that is all right. I could be there by say one o' clock in the afternoon then we need not rush things."

"Fine that will be excellent I look forward to it. See you Thursday at one o'clock then."

Andrew left the girls standing outside the Coach and Horses and waved as he turned the corner. Joan waved back whispering to Helen.

"He is so gorgeous you are so lucky having all that time with him on your own. You are so wicked and shameful."

Helen laughed. "Shameful that is good coming from you. There will be nothing going on I can assure you. I have no interest in him in that way. He is far too old for us."

"Nonsense he can only be about thirty years old. Besides I like older men."

"How do you know if you have never had one?"

"Well I know that I would. Anyway come on it is time that we were on our way."

They made their way back to Homelands both feeling that they had enjoyed the night even though they had discovered nothing really about Andrew. Inside Helen had been looking forward to the meeting with Andrew not for the same reasons of her friend Joan but the fact that he had been an important part of a family she had learned to call her own. She wanted to learn more about those two good people that had taken her in and showed so much love to her when no one else seemed to bother. Thursday came and she made her way to a house that once was her home a home that she had enjoyed for eight or more years, eight happy years and a place where she had felt safe. It would be the first time that she had returned there since that what appeared to her as the worst day of her life. It was the day that she was taken from there and placed at Homelands.

She had been looking forward but yet very nervous about this visit. Helen hardly knew this man that called himself Andrew and the son of her foster mother. She started to wonder if she could trust such a person, trusting him so much that she was entering a house alone.

She hesitated for a moment then knocked on the door a door that she would have just opened and walked in two years earlier but suddenly it didn't feel like home.

Andrew opened the door and smiled a welcome to Helen. Inside Helen saw that nothing in the house had changed since she had left.

Andrew asked her if she would like a cup of tea. Helen told him that she would love one.

He showed her into a room where she had spent many a long hour with her foster parents. In fact her chair was still in the position where she had left it. In the book shelf that was mounted on the wall stood some of her books that Mr. James had read to her on many occasions. She could feel herself filling up with emotion as she looked around the room.

Andrew returned with two cups of tea and set one down on a small table near to the chair that Helen had sat in.

"How are you today Helen?"

"Fine I am feeling fine. I have not been to see your mother today I am hoping to go there after we have finished. Have you been this morning?"

Andrew looked a little sheepish at the question.

"No I have been putting all this lot together for our meeting. I, like you am hoping to go later today. Anyway don't forget your tea. I have found some, well a lot to be exact, of photographs that you may like to see. The trouble is though once you start to look through photographs you can't stop and before you know where you are the morning has gone.

I must say though that I found some very early photographs of you and you have not changed much. Your facial features are just as they were when you were I take it eight or nine years of age." Helen blushed. "I don't like looking at myself I never have. I take an awful picture…

"Nonsense you have lovely features and have nothing to be ashamed of. I didn't mean to embarrass you in fact I saw it has a compliment." Andrew handed the photographs to Helen. Helen smiled at the first one that she remembered the actual day that it was taken.

"This was a very happy day and I thought at that time that my life was so good. We had so much fun that day."

Andrew felt happy and still inside a little sadness. "Yes I missed those days. We had so many when I was younger. Dad took me everywhere, fishing; football matches and of course birds watching. I remember him once buying me a bike and he borrowed his father's so that we could go cycling together. I tell you I have never laughed as much in all my life. That bike of my grandfather's it was so old and heavy compared with the modern bike that I had."

"Was it a penny farthing? I have seen those in pictures but I have never ridden one."

"No it was not quite as bad as that but I have to say that I felt embarrassed when we rode passed my mates in the village. I soon got over it though just being out in the countryside with my dad. I loved him so much you know."

"How old were you when you left for Australia?"

"I was eighteen a little young but I had no option but to leave."

Helen could not stop herself looking straight at Andrew.

"That is a big statement to make when you have just told me how much you loved being with your family. These photographs look at this one with your father. I would have said that there would be no way in which you could walk out of so much love."

Andrew sat back in the chair and did his best to hold back the tears that he could feel were trying to release themselves from inside his aching body.

"There is more to it than what there seems to be in those photographs. Like life under the skin of life often lies some deep unhappiness. I have carried that unhappiness for twelve years. I have, I felt that I had lost everything but I could not help what God had given me. I did hope that after a while that this would be seen but it wasn't."

"You say twelve years. How old are then?"

"Thirty two, well I am next week. Why do you ask?"

"No reason I just didn't know."

Helen hadn't meant to let it sound as though his age was important and had no idea why she had even asked him.

"Who is this with your father in the photograph?"

Andrew looked at the photograph that Helen was holding.

"Michael Parkinson, you know he is on the television."

"How did he know him?"

"They went to school together. Yes this was at one of the cricket matches on Shaw Lane. They both went to Barnsley Holgate Grammar School. They both loved cricket and Barnsley played on the pitches next to the school."

"Oh so, he was famous then?"

"I don't think so. He was known well he wanted to be famous for beating Brian Glover in the inter-house boxing matches. He told me many times about that."

"Who is Brian Glover?"

"Well he was a man of many parts. He was a wrestler and then he went into films a lot of films. He was on television. I think that he died though a few years ago."

"Did you ever meet any of them?"

"No, I felt that I had with the number of times dad told me and mother every time that Parkinson came on the television."

"Well he was proud not many people are friends with famous people are they?"

"Yes I can see why you would think that Helen. I can tell you that I wish that I had known my father later in my life. I knew him when I was a child but I would have loved to have known him as a person when I was an adult.

I could have done so much with him together. I can never bring those days back now. He's gone forever. I …. Sorry Helen I didn't think that I had so much unhappiness and sadness bottled up inside."

Helen hesitated at first then placed her arms around him.

"If you had been at home you and I could have been great friends. I have always wanted a bigger brother and it would have made my life complete Andrew. I do hope that we can become closer as foster brother and sister. I know that it would mean so much to your mother."

"Perhaps she stopped writing to me you know when I left for Australia. We were so close and although I loved my father my mother was always there for me.

Then all communications stopped and the last letter was so frightening for me even at nineteen years of age. I felt so alone and that is why I took solace by working with the Aborigines out in the bush."

"Why did she do that then? I can't understand it that was not the mother that I had learned to love. Your father was so good with me and the way they treated me I just thought that they had no children and I was someone that they had dreamed of. I feel sad now that I never knew that you existed, I honestly now feel awful about it."

"Nonsense it was not your fault. It was nobody's fault it was just the times perhaps if it had been today things could have been different."

"Why, what is different about today and then?"

"Just the amount of understanding and acceptance of"

"Acceptance of what though Andrew?"

Helen could see that Andrew was struggling with something. Inside he was fighting the fact that here was a girl who he had only known for hours and yet he was close to telling her this secret.

He knew that if his mother came from behind her memory loss that she might tell Helen anyway.

"I am gay Helen."

Helen was so shocked this was not the secret that she had been expecting. Stood there in front of her was the most tanned and handsome man who was not trying to tell her that he preferred men to women. She had no idea how to react.

"It's all right Helen I know it is a shock. I can tell you I didn't understand it myself and I can tell you I was scared stiff. I had no one to talk to about how I felt. I have never felt so alone in the whole of my life."

"When was it that you realised that you were well, gay?"

"I believe that I always knew but then I just thought it may be a phase hat boys go through."

"Didn't you like girls then?"

"Of course I did in fact I got on with girls better than boys. I felt safe and conversation was so easy. I think that the girls knew before I did."

"How did you parents feel then when they found out?"

Andrew took in a deep gasp intake of breath before he answered.

"It could have been better. The problem was that I had been building up the courage to tell them but I was too late."

"Too late, what do you mean?"

"I was beaten to it by a boy who had been bullying me and didn't like me very much. Yes I was bullied over it for years but I didn't allow it to upset me too much. In fact that was how it came out I finally gave way to my internal feelings and broke the bullies' nose. He then told his parents and they told mine. Of course they didn't believe them and when they asked me about it I told them that the boy was making it all up. However a week or so later I had to tell my mother."

"What did she say to you?"

"Well I have to admit she took it very well and gave me the biggest love. It felt so good after all those years of hiding my fear. It was always there even though my life at home was so happy."

"So why did you have to leave home?"

"Dad, he could not handle it. He told me that I had shamed him and that he could not live in the same house as a son that had betrayed him and his mother."

Helen felt sad and sorry inside. Even though she didn't really know Andrew she did know his father and he had never given her the impression that he could be so hard. There had to be something else that Andrew was not telling her.

"What did you do when he told you to get out then?"

"I had no plans I had not expected the reaction that I received. I was in total shock and I don't know to this day what I did at that moment. I remember looking at my mother but she covered her face so that I could not see I have never ever felt so alone, as I did at that time."

"Well you must have done something."

"Yes I suppose that I did. The first thing that I was aware of is being outside a friend's house. He still lived with his parents but I must have just walked there without knowing. I remember standing there and I was freezing cold and people kept looking at me as they passed by. I was so low I thought that I would be better if I died. Yes suicide was never far from my mind but that would have taken great strength and courage. I did not have either and I can tell you I was pleased that I didn't."

"That is awful Andrew how could you?"

"I know that today it seems rather foolish but I know how I felt. When I hear of people committing suicide it comes flooding back. I know exactly what they went through before they did what they did. No hope, no future just nothing more to live for."

"I am sorry but I still don't understand that sort of thinking. Nothing could be so bad that I could ever consider taking my own life. I know what it feels to be lonely Andrew and I don't think that there is anything worse than that. Oh yes I know people can be so sick and they know that the future will be just pain. I think that they would put up with that if they didn't know that although they were surrounded by love and kindness they were still on their own."

"If they had the love and the kindness around them surely that would help. I know that was all that I wanted in the years that followed."

"Yes it does help but inside you are still aware that you are the one that is dying and no one can feel that for you."

Andrew stopped talking and sighed deeply.

"You know Helen you are not just pretty but very acute in your thinking. Looking at the situation as it was then, you are right I missed that feeling of being hugged by my mother. Yes, even at that age a hug from someone you love is so important. My father was not one for giving you hugs, not at that age. When I was younger he did and I could still feel the warmth of those hugs and it was so sad, sad that I would never ever feel that sort of warmth again from my father."

Helen was running out of things that she could say to comfort this tanned and handsome man that sat there in front of her.

"Who was the friend that you went to see then?"

"Doctor Bellamy. Of course he was not a doctor then just a student but we were great friends."

"Was he aware that you were…?

"What gay you mean?"

"Well, yes."

"Yes he knew in fact he had warned me that there would be trouble if I didn't tell my parents. I knew that he was right, he normally was, but how do you tell someone, especially your parents that their son his gay."

"I can understand the dilemma that you were in but he was right. We should be able to talk to our parents about anything. I lost out on that. I didn't seem to have anyone that I could confide in. That was until I started to live with your parents. Your mother encouraged me to talk freely about any subject, yes even sex. Now I think I know where that came from. I think that both of them felt that they had let you down by not being open about life. I believe that it was only your father's pride that kept you apart.

From my dealings with them I think that if you had been in England then I think that the problem would have resolved itself. It would not be easy but time is a healer."

"It was the fact that aids and the effects on people was in the news and I think that they were so scared. Twelve years is not a long time but people's perception of things, do change. I felt that dad would never forgive me and that I could not have dealt with that."

"Well we will never know now. I do hope that your mother pulls out of this and that you and she can find the love that you both had for all those years."

"Bless you Helen I wish with all my heart that this could happen. In fact we both have things I am sure that we would like to say to her."

Again silence fell over the two for a moment.

"Did you say that you had found some papers about my back ground?"

"Oh yes, I found them in a box where mum keeps the insurance policies. If I had not met you I would have not known what they were. The people named in there I have no knowledge of and at first they didn't make sense."

"Names, you say. What were they?"

"Did you know anyone called Hackforth?"

"Yes I was fostered with them for about a year or so just before I came to live with your mother and father."

"You had better have the papers then perhaps they may help you in finding whatever it is that you are looking for Helen. There is an address in there so you may wish to visit them."

"I think that they may have moved from there. Mrs. Freeman has been trying to contact them for me but they had moved from the home where I stayed. She found out that one of her son's had been deeply involved with drugs and had gone to prison. They seem to have disappeared but Mrs. Freeman is still trying."

"Another son that has become a disappointment to his parents what fools we all are."

"No we are not and neither are you. He had a choice in what he did but you didn't. That is the big difference Andrew so you try and forgive yourself. You are not an evil man and any father would be proud to have a son like you. Anyway I have to go if I am going to see your mother. I have enjoyed our conversation and thank you for showing me those photographs."

"My pleasure Helen we must do this again and soon. If I can find out any more information for you I will contact you at Homelands if you don't mind."

"No that would be good. Any information that can help me find out where I came from would be welcome."

"Tell mum that I will be along tonight. I know that I have you to thank for the fact that I can talk to her. We don't know if she will be well enough to come home but I am waiting for the doctors to tell me. Apparently they have a progress meeting every two weeks and a monthly meeting when decisions are made on each and every patient. Maybe then we can make some plans for the future."

They said their goodbyes and Helen left the home she had known for some eight years or so. The homeliness was still not there. She knew that it was the people that made a home not the bricks and mortar.

Chapter Six

Two weeks had passed since Helen and Andrew had met at his mother's home. There had been no news regarding the release of Mrs. James from the hospice. Joan and Helen had discussed many things but as yet the fact that Andrew had told Helen that he was gay had not entered any part of the conversation. Helen didn't see that she had a right to break the confidence that Andrew had placed on her. It was often made very difficult when her best friend kept talking about seeking some sort of relationship with him.
"You know Helen I believe that Andrew has returned to England to seek a bride. I could be that bride I could easily adapt to living in the outback amongst those Aborigines. Rolf Harris seemed to enjoy their culture so I think that I could."

"You live where there are no shops I don't think so Joan not you, you would not last a fortnight out there."

"Don't you think so Helen even with a man like him?"

"Not even with George Clooney. I know you and living in the desert is not one of the best ideas you have had."

"I suppose that you are right. You know you have so much common sense it makes me so mad. Why do you always look at things so coolly I want to jump in with both feet and then think about what I am doing?"

"He could just be a friend you know. You do not have to fall madly in love with every man that you meet. One day Mr. Right will come along and you will know it is right. You will make a good wife and a good mother so just is patient."

"Helen Taylor I love you. How have I managed to live my life without you? I know that my life has been one crisis after another. Now I do have my feet firmly on the ground."

The following day Helen had gone off to work and Joan was walking in the grounds when she saw Andrew walking up the long drive towards the house. She called out and he walked over to her.

"Hello Andrew how lovely to see you."

"It is nice to see you Joan. How are you I hope that you are keeping well?"

"Yes I am fine Andrew thank you. Are you looking for Helen?"

"Well yes I was just wondering if she had heard anymore about the Hackforth's."

"She is out at work but we could walk around the grounds for a while if you would like to she will be home about two o'clock."

"Fine that would be nice. You can tell me about you and your friend Helen. I feel that I have known you for so long and yet I don't know anything about you both."

They walked slowly through the grounds until they came to the seat where Helen and Joan had sat on many occasions since they became friends.

"Shall we sit here Andrew this is where Helen and I have many heart to heart discussions about life?"

"I bet that they were interesting conversations Joan."

"I wouldn't say that but they were very helpful for both of us so yes we would say that they were significant."

They both sat down under the large old oak tree.

"Tell me about yourself Joan if you do not mind."

"No I don't mind. My life would not be what I could call interesting. I think that you may find it boring after your life out in Australia."

"My life is not that exciting Joan, believe me."

"Well I was born in a place called Grimethorpe in Yorkshire. Do you know it?"

"Yes, but I have not been there for many years. I remember my father taking me to a park or something to listen to a brass band there once."

"Yes that's right my father was in the band for many years. He played the cornet and took pride in the number of competitions that they took part in and won."

"Does your father still play in the band Joan?"

"No he died about eight years ago now. He still played up to then. "

"Died, you say your father died?"

"In a way he did. Yes we were involved in an accident and my mother was killed and my father very badly injured. It would have been better if he had died....

Joan started to cry at this point and Andrew placed his arms around her. Joan snuggled into the chest of Andrew and felt good.

"Are you all right then Joan? You don't have to tell me if it is going to upset you."

"No I don't mind. He is still alive but he is in a home. He doesn't know anyone and he is wheelchair bound. This means nothing though because he never gets out of bed unless the nurses make him."

"That is such a shame what did you do then Joan? How old were you then?"

"Ten, I was just ten years of age."

"Ten what a pity tell me about your father Joan." Joan sighed deeply, which she did every time that she had to think of her family.

"He was a very principled man but his principles often got him into trouble. He stood up for everything that he felt was important."

"There is nothing wrong with that is there?"

"Not if the cost is not too high. My mother gave him love and always supported him even though the cost to her and me was sometimes too high. I often heard my mother crying but she tried her best not to let my father or I see her.

My father took solace with the colliery band and this helped him but that left a lot of time for my mother to have to come to terms with weeks of having no money and bailiffs coming to the door."
"Bailiffs you say. Were things that bad?"
"Oh yes I know that I was very young but I was old enough to know when my mum was upset."
"Yes I can understand that Joan. Didn't your father work then?"
"Yes he worked down the pit from being fifteen years of age. Then he had a good job but I know it was hard because he was so tired when he came home from the pit. He took coal from the face and we burned it on the fire. We all had to tell my class at school what our fathers did for a living. A lot of my class didn't know but I asked my mum and she told me about the coal and why it was important for us all."
"I don't understand then why you were so poor if he had such a hard but hard job."

"He was always going on strike over something or the other according to my mum. He was what they called a union shop steward. They looked after the members of the union so that the bosses didn't treat them badly. I told you that he was a man of strong principles and he would stand up even though he was making trouble for himself. He used to tell us that the bosses didn't like him but he would say that he didn't have a problem with that."

"Well there is nothing wrong with having strong principles and if he was looking after the rights of the men he should have been congratulated."

"Well that was all right whilst the unions were very strong but then came the big strike. I was only two years old but I remember the trouble that it caused. I remember a man called Arthur Scargill coming to our home with some other men and they were planning all sorts. My mum would take me out so that they could talk but I knew that something was wrong. The voices sounded so mad when they spoke of some people. It would seem that whilst a lot of people were on strike some didn't stop working and there were fights in the streets."

"I remember that they said that it got that bad that son was against father and father against son, neighbour against neighbour depending on the beliefs. It was so sad that complete close communities became war zones.

The pictures on the television were showing the police and these desperate men fighting in the street. They said that it was a political strike and Margaret Thatcher was the Prime minister at the time. She made the decision to take on the union and there could only be one winner in that situation.

It was so sad that they could not talk and sort whatever it was around a table. The fact that it was a war well we know what the results were of that conflict. More pits closed and so many men became jobless by this action."

"Yes that was out trouble the bosses wanted an excuse, any excuse to get rid of my father. He was not a man that would beg and although those he had tried to protect some stood by him others just ignored him. He was such a proud man and as I grew older and started to understand I knew that he was churning inside as people turned their back on him and his family.

The problem was that a lot of those who insisted that they were not going to strike were hounded so much that some actually committed suicide. They could not take the hassle and the attack on their homes and their families. The children were bullied at school and the homes had paint daubed all over them. The name was scab and that still exists even today eight years on. Some of those very close communities have now broken up as the pits closed. The effect was not just felt by those men but their wives were totally ignored within the community. The fact that once each one helped everybody else and now it had turned to what it did was just unbelievable. It was and still isn't a happy situation."

"You and your family survived though didn't you?"

"Well I suppose that we did. I remember that mum was taking in washing and doing housework for those people who could afford it and were not involved with the miners' strike. It was hard I went to school with holes in my shoes covered by cardboard. I felt so ashamed but I knew that my parents were doing the best that they could.
I also noted a change in my father he dropped his union job as the members lost their jobs and he blamed himself for their plight. He took a job with the council anything that would bring in some money to try and support his family. I told you that he was a very strong principled man and he did not even attempt to collect anything from the dole. He told my mother on several occasions that it was

government money and he would not lower himself to accept their charity."

"But that was not charity he had earned it when he was working."

"Yes but he didn't see it like that. He had a little bit of redundancy money but they paid him the minimum that they could get away with. That all went out on paying the bills that had built up during the strike. I didn't know this then but my mother told me all about that time in their lives when I got a little older. She thought that it was important that I remembered the hard times that they endured to try and save the pits and thus the livelihoods of all those villagers and the families."

Were there any close friends of your family that shared different views on the strike? You know what I mean they became scabs as they were called?"

"Yes my mother's best friend."

"What happened to her then?"

"The Elliot's this family had lived in the village forever. There were three generations living in the village at that time. The Elliot's were once a loving family they went on holiday together all the time. My mother's friend was pregnant when the strike started and she was having problems. I didn't know this at the time but mum told me later when one day I came in on a conversation between a neighbour and my mother. Anyway she apparently had been diagnosed with some sort of cancer and needed an operation but she was not going to risk losing their first child. The doctors tried to convince her that she needed the operation and the treatment if they were to save her life. She would not give way at all. My mother gave her so much support through this. The treatment that she was on wasn't covered by the National Health and they were paying privately for it. From what I gathered later on if they didn't pay then the treatment stopped and the end was inevitable. Anyway when the time for the strike came her husband who was also a close friend of my father could not afford to be out of work. The unions would not pay the strikers apparently they didn't have the money. He wanted the treatment to carry on and that meant that she had to have decent food to enable her to keep the strength for the treatment and the new baby."

"I can understand him wanting that couldn't you Joan?"

"I suppose so but as I said I didn't know about it until many years later. Then it was all history."

"What happened then Joan?"

Well when he refused to join the strike there was a great deal of understanding for them. Besides Arthur Scargill and the union had told everyone that Maggy Thatcher would cave in like Ted Heath had done some years earlier. Unfortunately that didn't happen and the longer it went on the more people became desperate. There were no food in the homes and no money for anything like bills.

Soon that understanding turned to anger as these families enjoyed food and having money in their pockets. It was not long before trouble came and these men had to be taken by bus and police escort into the pits for their own safety. The trouble then turned to the families of those men and their homes.

Everyone had lost any sympathy and it just turned so nasty. In the end he could take no more and Mr. Elliot committed suicide. The final straw was that his own father turned against him. He had offered all their savings to take care of the treatment but that would run out within four weeks and he couldn't take the risk of the strike still being on after that time."

"God that was awful, his own father helping to drive him to suicide. How on earth could he live with himself?"

"The fact was that he didn't. After the strike was driven into the ground he also took his own life.

That family suffered so much and it achieved exactly nothing, for all those other families whether they worked or were on strike. Everyone lost their livelihoods and that was the biggest shock for all."

"What happened to the wife then did she have her baby?"

"I am not sure she left the village after her husband died and seemed to disappear. She didn't but she was the wife of a scab so no one cared. How uncaring was that. I feel so ashamed that something like that could result in that sort of behaviour."

"Well perhaps you will be the generation that allows those differences to die along with the trouble."

"I would like to think so but I doubt that very much. The lasting effect of that time in 1984 was written into history and so will always be present. In fact it is always brought up when any of the other so-called strong unions threaten strike. No that time changed things forever and all those close communities disappeared and will never ever be replaced. In fact I believe that it is for this reason that communities now are not communities at all. The rouble that they find themselves in with vandalism and worse is purely due to the fact that no one cares for their neighbour anymore."

"You know Joan I can agree with that. You know if the Aborigines lived like modern day England they would not survive. They need each other and that is what keeps them alive.

You have a clever brain for someone so young."

"Young I am not that young. There are only a few years between you and me."

"There are more than just a few Joan."

"Anyway what happened to your father after the strike?"

Joan wiped a tear away from her eye. She hadn't spoken of those family problems for many years and not to a stranger such as Andrew.

"Well the strike was over after a year but the problems are still present to this very day. People learn to adapt to the new situations something gets lost along the way but life does go on. He as I told you found a job with the council it wasn't much but it paid money into some very empty pockets. He settled into it for about two and a half years and then he found a job in the steel industry.
Apparently I heard him telling my mother that he had been approached to try and become a shop steward. Mother put her foot down in no uncertain terms and that was that. Things began to get better and laughter returned back into our home something that had not been present for many years.
Then dad won some money on something they ran at his works and he bought us a car. We thought that this was great. We had never owned a car before and not many owned on around where we lived.

Dad was so proud and he took us around the countryside every weekend. We had picnics and I could see that mum was really happy and that made me feel happy inside. I must admit I had a great deal of reservations about our family happiness could it last. Those black days of 1984 to 1987 had left a sort of negatives about life, which was hard to shake off."

"What about your mother's friend who was having the baby did your mother ever find out where she went?"

"No I don't think so. Her name was never brought up in front of me anyway. I did hear someone tell my dad that he had blood on his hands with the number of people that had died during and after the strike. I think that this had some sort of effect on him. He was not a bad man but I think that he did feel a little guilty about some of the things that took place."

"What the scabs and the effect it had on their families?"

"Oh no not them he had no feelings at all about those people. I know that it sound un- Christian but he believed that they had allowed those people to take away not just the livelihood of their neighbours but also the pride of those people."

"So life was looking up then Joan."

"Yes it was but I still had awful feeling inside about the future."

"What happened then Joan?"

"Well life carried on getting better and believe it or not my father became a manager the one thing that he had fought against all his early young life. However he felt that he had not relinquished any of his own principles. He would treat those who he managed like they were important to the business as they were."

"That is very commendable of him I would have liked to meet him."

Jane lowered her head as the tears came forward.

"Sorry Joan I didn't mean to upset you."

Joan shook her head and she felt one of his arms touch her on her shoulder.

"That will not be possible."

"Why he isn't dead his he, not another casualty of the strike?"

"No he is not dead but he is as good as dead."

Andrew screwed his face up trying to understand what Joan meant by her statement.

"It happened in 1993 we were on our way to the first real holiday for some years. We were going to Blackpool for a week's holiday. We were just outside Preston when a lorry ran into us my father swerved the car to try and miss it but it ploughed into the passenger side. My mother was killed outright and my father trapped as the engine came out of the front of the car. I was thrown forward but managed to come away uninjured."

"God that is terrible. What did you think at the time then Joan? I know that you told me that you had this awful feeling inside about the future."

"I didn't think of it at the time I was too engrossed by the death of my mother and the injuries the almost fatal injuries that my father had sustained. My future, in my own mind I had no future the fact that the most important person in my life had gone and the second was almost certain to be a cripple how do you come from that situation believing that you have a future. I was ten years old who was going to take care of me. Who was I going to talk to when I wanted help?"

"Yes but your father was still alive Joan yes he may be a cripple but you still had him to turn to."

"No Andrew you don't understand he was ill not just in his body but his mind. He blamed himself for my mother's death and he could not take that. He sank lower and lower even the doctors couldn't find a solution. Don't you recognise what I am saying? Your mother has done exactly the same thing. She gave up like my father she had more to live for like you but worse than that she had Helen who loved her very much. She deserted her like my father deserted me all those years ago.

People in the village started to say that he had been cursed for all the trouble and distress that he had caused many people during that bloody strike. They could have been right because so many people were ruined by it and someone had to be responsible."

"But yes I can see what you mean but surely the strike was bigger than just your father."

"I have told him that many times Andrew. I, like you and Helen, have been visiting my father in the hospital for so long. I have sat there with him for hours talking about mother about me and telling him to forgive himself. I just want him back he's my father and I love him. I need my father more now than when I was a child."

"So you were ten when the accident happened where did you go surely they didn't place you in a home?"

"No I had an auntie she took me in for a while. I don't remember the early days I was still in shock from the accident. Oh everyone showed me plenty of pity but it did not help me. How could they understand what I was going through? Here I was a ten year old girl whose mother had been taken away and her father who had lost his ability to walk. I disliked everyone but most of all I hated God for what he had done to my family. My auntie was a very religious woman and my uncle was a lay preacher. They did not like it when I told them that I hated God. They threatened that if I didn't change my attitude that they could no longer give me a roof over my head. Blasphemy was not allowed in this their home."

"How did that make you feel then Joan?"

"Sad but later I did come to understand where she was coming from. They had four other children so the pressure on my uncle and auntie must have been hard. Having four children is bad enough but then to have another thrust on you who attacked the most important thing in your life. Well it can't have been easy. Religion was their way of life it had always been that way their children believed in the same things and here was I pulling that ideology down. No I can now understand their feelings."
"But surely they has Christians could see that you were having your own little hell. If it is not up to Christians to help anyone in that situation I don't know what is."
"Perhaps you are right Andrew but my uncle well he tried during the strike to help but no one listened."
"Hadn't you any other relatives that could have taken you in perhaps who had a little better understanding of what your needs were?"

"No my mother's sister died of meningitis when she was six years of age. So there was only my father's brother and his wife…

"You mean that the uncle you were living with was your father's brother?"

"Yes his younger brother. They used to be very close but the strike put paid to that relationship. I told you that my uncle tried to help I could remember the times when he came round to talk to my father. They always finished up having a blazing row over the cruel way in which this strike was being carried out. I can remember my father shouting at his brother not to come preaching in his house. I was so afraid you know and so young then. It didn't stop there though even after the strike had fallen apart they still argued over the rights and wrongs. When I was about seven years old I remember my uncle calling at the homes of different villagers trying to get them to forgive each other but they just basically threw him out.

In fact mindless vandals in the depth of the night attacked my uncle's home. They painted scab lover all over the walls they knew that this was not true because he gave help to those that were on strike when he could. They provided meals and clothing for the children but that was all forgotten. I tell you that bloody strike whether justified or not had a lot to answer for."

Andrew tried his best to comfort Joan without getting too close. He was remembering her words earlier about the age difference and had a feeling that she was looking at him, not in a way that he wanted her to.

"I don't know what to say Joan. This couple who I thought were treating you shamelessly and without any Christian understanding seem to be good people."

"They were and they still are despite it all. Some people mainly young men that weren't even about during the strike still occasionally confront them.

They call them names they are just bullies that can only live off their father's hate. Who can go around giving hassle to sixty years old men? There were a lot who tried to help a lot of people that were in real trouble and they received nothing in return, neither did they want it."

"What happened to you then Joan did things settle down for you after a while?"

"Not really I was only with my auntie and uncle for about six months. She became ill and had all to look after her own four children never mind one that hated God. No I had come home from school one day and there in the house were two people I had not seen before. They were talking to my auntie and uncle in the front room. They called me in and told me to sit down. Inside I was shaking with fear as all the different things rushed through my head. What had I done? Who were these people, was I going to be punished, but what for?

After a while my auntie told me that the two ladies were social workers that were going to help me. They were going to make sure that I had a happy home where someone would make me very happy like I used to be. I started to cry, no sob. I told them that I was sorry if I had caused them any trouble and I didn't really hate God. I just want to stay with you auntie."

"What did your auntie say to that then?"

Joan started to tremble, she thought that all this was behind her but it was obviously lay dormant deep inside her for all those years. She had felt some of it when she had been telling Helen when they first met. This however felt different here she was laying her life out to a somewhat stranger. She suddenly felt naked in front of this man. Yes she fancied the pants off him but was she ready to tell all to him.

"Are you all right Joan? Perhaps you could do with a walk we have been sat here for some time and I know my backside feels a little numb."

"Yes that would be good. I need to walk we could go back towards the house perhaps Helen has arrived back by now."

"Do you know that I had completely forgotten why I had come here Joan that story that you have been telling me is fascinating. I thought that I had been badly treated but you… well that is something else."

"I am sorry if I have laid a heavy burden on you Andrew. It is not something that I make a habit of and in fact I feel rather foolish that I have told you so much about myself. I don't know anything about you apart from what Helen has told me and that is not a lot."

"Well that can soon be put straight Joan. I can tell you something about me as we walk back to the

house. There are like everybody a few skeletons in my cupboard but nothing that I am ashamed of."
Andrew told Joan how he had gone over to Australia and had found a friend who told him about the job out in the outback working with the Aborigines. He told her how he had settled out there and now had a house and a lot of friends. He omitted to tell her about the fact that he was gay. He didn't feel that it was appropriate at that moment.

He told her how devastated he was to learn that his father had died and his mother had been taken ill. He reflected on what Joan had told him about her feelings when she felt alone. He told her that he had felt and still did, exactly in the same way that she had felt.

Joan listened with part of her mind whilst the other was still going over those past parts of her life that she had managed to rediscover whilst sat under that old oak tree.

She remembered her and Helen wondering what things that old oak tree had seen and overheard over those hundreds of years. Then she thought that it had heard her story or at least some of it. Finally they were stood outside of the house. Joan stopped and looked at Andrew.

"Again I apologise for laying this at your doorstep Andrew. I have never told anyone of some of those things that I have told you."

"It is all right Joan. I am pleased that you have shown that you trust me enough to tell me those things. I can relate in many ways to how you feel because I have had similar things happen to me. Perhaps we should write a book about it who knows we could have a best seller."

They both smiled at the thought.

"I don't know who would play me if they made a film of it Andrew. Then who would want to pay to see a thing like that? People go out to be cheered up not to be made miserable."

"I think that a lot of people would. I bet there are hundreds of people out there that feel that they are the only ones that have been treated in the way that we have. Anyway look it is too late now to see Helen. If you could tell her that I will call on her another day I would be very much obliged. Thanks again for today Joan it is a privilege to know you. I will see you again I am sure. Bye."

Joan watched him leave and with her head down in her chest she made her way back into the house. At that moment all she wanted to do is to be in her room by herself.

Chapter Seven

The following weeks saw Helen and Joan's relationship growing closer they had enrolled in a charity that tried to improve the living standards of people especially the children out in Zambia. Helen knew about these charities through Mrs. James. She and Mr. James organised functions around the village to enable the charity to raise funds to buy medical equipment and blankets to send out there. Joan joined Helen at first just to have something to do but later became more and more involved.

They were running a Bring and Buy sale at the local hall and things were going very well. Helen and Joan had become a very good team and everybody praised them for the input.

During a rest period Joan asked Helen if she had seen Andrew lately.

"Yes I had lunch with him the other day after we had been visiting his mother."

"No news then as to whether they are going to allow her home?"

"No I think that they are waiting a little longer to see that the improvement continues. She still does not remember either Andrew or me. Oh she knows that we visit her a lot but she is not sure as to why, not as yet."

Did Andrew speak of me then Helen?"

"He told me that you and he had talked for a long time the other week. I didn't know that he had been to Homelands to see you."

"He didn't he came to see you but you were out. We just walked around the grounds and talked. We sat on out seat under the old oak tree. He asked about my background but that was all."

"What did you tell him?"

"Well I told him how we as a family battled through the miner's strike of 1984 the fact that what the strike did to break up family and friends. Then I told him about the car accident and the fact that my mother was killed and my father crippled. He asked what happened to me then and I spoke of the time that I spent at my auntie's. He seemed quite interested I thought that he wanted to learn more about me maybe he wants to have some sort of relationship with me, I don't know. I expected to hear from him again but I never did. Perhaps it is you he is interested in, and not I. That is the story of my life always the bridesmaid never the bride."

"I can assure that is not the case Joan. I think that you will find that he has no interest in either of us."

"What do you mean Helen? Why shouldn't he have any interest in us, aren't we good enough for him?"

Helen hesitated she didn't want to break the confidentiality that Andrew had placed on her by telling her that he was actually gay.

"Perhaps he thinks that we are not good enough for him Helen. I didn't think that he was like that I thought from how we talked that he enjoyed my company. I can understand that he must feel close to you because of the love that his mother had for you but I…

"No Joan you are wrong he doesn't show any interest other than a friend because…."

Again Helen hesitated.

"Go on Helen because what?"

"Because he is gay there I have said it but please don't tell Andrew that I have told you, promise me."

Joan could not utter anything never mind a promise. She showed total shock of all the things that she had been thinking Andrew being gay was not one of them.

Helen's attention was taken away by an old lady asking about some jugs at the far end of the table. Helen didn't want to go away from Joan until she had been given that promise but the old lady was insistent.

"Hello love didn't you once live with Mrs. James?"

Now it was Helen's turn to look shocked.

"Excuse me I'm sorry I was thinking of something else love. What was it you said?"

"I said didn't you once live with a Mrs. James in Dodworth near Barnsley?"

Helen looked astonished that someone here in Doncaster should be at this Bring and Buy sale that actually remembered her from Dodworth.

"Yes I did but how did you know? How could you possibly remember that?"

"I lived next door she was my neighbour for thirty years. My two sons and daughters used to spend time with them especially after their son Andrew left home to go to Australia. They were so upset about his leaving you know, they would never speak of it to anyone. Andrew's father took to my eldest son and they went bird watching together, they both loved their hobby. My son used to sketch the birds for him you know. He works in London now he illustrates for National Geographic. The work that he does for them is important to him and the fact that he loves doing it makes it a bonus. He just loves sketching all those wild creatures in the environment that they live in.

When my children left home I missed them so much but Mr. and Mrs. James were good to me they were always good neighbours. Then you came along a small nervous child that looked so sorrowful and unhappy. You took ages to settle in and I used to show you some of the pictures that my son had sketched you loved them so much. I gave you one of a small lion cub do you remember?"

"Mrs. Burns isn't it?"

"Yes love you do remember. Yes that picture was one of the first that our Timothy drew he was so proud of it."

"I still have that picture Mrs. Burns. I had forgotten all about it until I was searching for an old photograph and I found it. I was not sure where I had got it from though.

Didn't you move from next door to Mrs. James?"
"Yes I moved here to Doncaster to live with my eldest daughter. She works at the General Hospital here in Doncaster. Yes I have been here for about six or seven years now."
"You must have a good memory to recognise me after all that time. I must be honest I didn't remember you at first."
"Well love you were only about ten years of age then and I told you that you were a very unhappy child. How long did you stay with Mrs. James?"
"Eight years."
"Eight years, why did you leave there they were a very kind couple?"
"Mr. James died and Mrs. James became very ill she couldn't cope so I moved here to Doncaster."
The old lady looked shocked although she had always intended to keep in touch time had taken its toll and that intention had gone.

"That is such a shame my Timothy will be so upset when I tell him. How is Mrs. James now then?"
"Still ill but she is a lot better than she was. They thought that she was going to die."
"Die whatever was it that she was suffering from. It wasn't cancer was it?"
"No they called it a broken heart after she lost her husband."
"Well it does happen love they don't understand the mind like they should and broken hearts occur a lot more than it is given credit for."
"I go and see her at every opportunity and I have seen a great deal of improvement. Her eyes were so sad when I first visited her but they are bright and a lot happier now. Her son Andrew is back over here from Australia and he is visiting her."
"So he should, I tell you they were so upset when he upped and left. Is he back for good now then?"
"I don't know he hasn't said what his plans are, not to me anyway."

"About these jugs love how much are they?"
Helen took a deep breath to try and bring her thought back to the Bring and Buy sale.
"The large one is fifty pence and the two smaller ones are twenty five pence each."
The old lady smiled at Helen.
"You wouldn't let me have the lot for sixty pence would you? I'm sorry I don't remember your name."
"It's Helen and yes that will be all right. Do you collect jugs then?"
"Oh yes I have shelves and cupboards full. My daughter luckily is also an avid collector so she doesn't bother that we have so many. Her husband Brian, well he doesn't say much but I don't think he is amused. In fact I think that he thinks we are nuts."
"Well I will look out for more for you we often take a lot in before the sales."

"That is very kind of you Helen. It has been lovely seeing you again. Give my regards to Mrs. James when you next visit her will you."

The old lady left and Joan rushed across to talk to Helen. She had been bursting to break in on Helen's conversation with the old lady.

"What did you say to me? Did you say that Andrew is gay?"

Helen shook her head. "I am afraid so Joan so you see that it is not you or me that is the problem."

Joan still could not believe what she heard Helen telling her. How could the tanned handsome young man be anything other than a ladies' man? No Helen had to want him for herself but why would her best friend say these lies.

"I don't believe you Helen I would know if he was I am not a fool you know."

"I was as shocked as you are Joan. When he told me I couldn't think of a word to say. I must have looked a fool myself sat there with my mouth open."

"When did he tell you? I didn't think that you were that close the two of you."

"He just came out with it when I went to his mother's house to go through some of the papers that he had found. He was explaining why he had left home and gone off to Australia. Apparently it was his father that turned him out of his home. He never forgave him for bringing that sort of shame on to his mother and father."

"But what shame people understand more these days. No one would have looked at his parents and said that they had failed."

"Perhaps not today but twelve years ago things would have been a great deal different. Andrew told me how he had been bullied and called names can you imagine the effect that would have had on his mother if she had known."

"Why did he tell them then?"

"According to Andrew his mother somehow guessed but they both decided to keep it away from his father for the time being. However someone made fun of something that Andrew's father had said. When he challenged the man he spilt the beans by telling Andrew's father that how could anyone take notice of a man who breeds queers. Andrew's father was not a violent man but he hit this man and then became doubly ashamed. Ashamed that he had actually lost his temper and hit this man and that his son had never told him about being gay."

"Why would it have made a difference do you think?"

"I don't know but I don't suppose any man would not feel like Andrew's father felt if he heard what he heard in that way. Can you imagine your father… sorry?

"No go on Helen it is all right."

"Well if your father heard while he was out having a drink in the pub that his beloved daughter was a drug addict or worse still a drug pusher."

"No I can't I could only imagine. He hated it when they showed it on the television news and stories of the criminal activities that the 'druggies' got up top to feed their habit. He used to say that he would slap them in jail and throw away the key. Those that attacked old people to steal their money well he would say they wanted hanging."

"He didn't like them then?"

Joan and Helen laughed.

"I know that it is not a laughing matter but you see what I mean about Andrew's father."

Inside Joan was still puzzled why it was that Andrew had never mentioned the fact that he was gay when they had that talk weeks ago. He knew that she had feelings for him. She felt that she ought to teach him a lesson but that would just be creating a vendetta that would not solve anything.

"What did the old lady want then Helen she seemed to be in deep conversation with you? I thought that she was never going to leave."

"Well she wanted those green jugs apparently she and her daughter collect jugs. I told her that if we got anymore in that we would save them for her."

"So all that talk was about jugs then?"

"Oh no she told me that she knew me. Yes she lived next door to Mrs. James at Dodworth."

"She has come a long way hasn't she just for a Bring and Buy sale?"

"No she now lives here in Doncaster. She moved in with her daughter and her husband. One of her sons was a big friend of Andrew's father. They became friends when Andrew had gone off to Australia. He now works for National Geographic and goes all over the world."

"Did she know that Mrs. James is ill then?"

"No she left over ten years ago."

"Ten years how did she recognise you then you could have only been about ten."

"I have no idea she told me that it was my face because she couldn't remember my name."

"Did you recognise her?"

"Not at first but then she told me about a drawing that her son had given me. Can you remember when I was looking for that photograph you picked up that drawing of a lion cub?"

"Yes I remember it was very good I didn't say anything but I thought that you may have drawn it."

"You are joking I have no talent in that direction I wish that I had. No as soon as she told me about that I remembered her name, Mrs. Burns. Isn't it a small world though all those people and she has to come to our Bring and Buy stall and I have to serve her."

"Life is strange I don't think that I will ever be surprised by what I see or hear especially when you told me about Andrew. I still can't believe it although inside I know that you wouldn't lie to me about a thing like that."

"I hope that you do Joan how could you think that I would make something up like that?"

"I didn't say you had made it up. I just said that it was hard to believe. You must have thought that when you found out."

Helen thought back to that day when Andrew had told her and knew that Joan was right.

"No I didn't believe it Joan."

"Tell you what Helen I know that Mrs. Freeman doesn't like it but why don't we share a bottle of wine tonight after we have finished here. I need something to help me absorb all these things."

Helen laughed. "You mean nothing of the kind. You know that we both like a glass of wine but if you want an excuse to have two bottles then I am up for it."

They had the hall where they held the Bring and Buy sale until three o'clock in the afternoon. The hall then changed to a fitness club so they had to ensure that they had the tables cleared away before then.

The charity had loaned a small backroom where they could keep the tables and some of the unsold items so this was very convenient more than having to cart it all away in Helen's small car. Neither Helen nor Joan had any inclines to join the fitness club they had on occasions stayed to watch but had never been enthused to join. The ages of the regulars were mostly sixty and seventy years of age. Both Helen and Joan were amazed how fit these old people were.

"I hope that when I get to their age I will be able to bend and stretch like they do. I think it is wonderful that they have the energy to do it. Where do they find it all from Helen?"

"I have no idea but I could do with some of what they are on."

They made their way back to Homelands calling on the way to the supermarket and bought two bottles of red wine. They both preferred red to white as both suffered from heartburn and acid when they drank the white wine.

There were no rules, well not specific rules that forbade drink in the rooms. The only mention was for the younger girls who at sixteen and seventeen were regarded as under age for drinking. Helen and Joan knew that some did sneak drink into their rooms because they had when they were sixteen but managed never to get caught.

Boys however were not allowed within the premises at all. Visitors that are men, like Andrew could sit in the lounges and talk, but were not allowed into the rooms of the girls.

They both decided that they would have a shower and then by that time it would be teatime and then when tea was over they could go back to Joan's room and have a quiet drink.

Joan was keen to learn more about Andrew from Helen and thought that with a little drink inside her she may tell her more than she had about this man of mystery.

Tea was over and they had settled in and were having a glass of wine, which got to two and then three. Both were feeling merry but no drunk and both were getting very talkative.

"Tell me Helen, are you still a virgin?"

Helen looked shocked and yet managed to smile at the question. She knew that this was not a subject that either would have spoken of if they had not had a drink or two.

"Well it is a straight forward question. Are you still a virgin?"

"Yes of course I am. I have never really had a boyfriend and I certainly don't go in for one-night stands. Why aren't you?"

Joan shrugged her shoulders.

"I am not sure."

Helen laughed. "You must know if you have had it or haven't surely."

"No I don't know whether I have or have not had it and that is the truth."

Helen took another drink and poured some more wine into Joan's glass.

"I don't understand why you can't know. Did someone rape you or something? Did he take advantage whilst you were drunk or asleep?"

Joan placed her glass on the small table.

Well you remember I told you that I used to live with my auntie and uncle but after awhile they couldn't cope so I was placed with some foster parents in the next village."

"Yes I remember are you…?

"No I was at first upset with my auntie for letting me go to complete strangers. I was so mad that I thought of running away but I could not think as to where I could go. I managed after a while to settle as much as you do. They were not a bad couple and treated me well but the rejection by my own blood had still taken its toll on my mind."

"I can imagine that Joan you poor thing."

"They had two sons one who was three years younger than me and the other about the same age perhaps a few months older. He, well both of the boys were not bad looking. I began getting feelings for the older boy and I knew that he liked me. His younger brother would get very jealous because his brother always wanted to be with me. He couldn't understand why his brother preferred to play with a girl rather than him."

"What do you mean that you got feelings for this boy how old were you then?"

"Fifteen going on sixteen he would come to my room and we would play cards and video games. The younger brother used to barge in but his

brother would push him out and this made my relationship with the younger brother harder.
Then one day he suggested taking our clothes off to play another game that he had been told about at school. I did not like it I had never taken my clothes off in front of a boy before. Anyway after a while we took some of our clothes off and he showed me the game."

"What game? What was it called?"

"Doctors and nurses apparently we had to touch parts that were called out. He would say a name and I had to touch it on his body. Then I would say something and he touched it on mine."

"Sounds a strange game to me Joan I have never heard of such a game."

"I hadn't but it seemed harmless I still had my bra and knickers on so it was just like being at the swimming pool really."

"So was it then that you think that you had sex?"

"Oh no, sometime later we started to play this game regularly it was a better game than the video games. Then one day we decided to take everything off and I realised that boys were different to girls in many ways.

I found the fact that he touched parts of my body and I became very excited. I trembled with excitement and so did he. His thing used to stand upright and was so hard. He asked me to touch it and at first I was frightened but he slowly placed my hand on it and it felt good. He pushed my hand up and down it and suddenly white stuff shot out and went all over me. I thought I had damaged him but he was so breathless. He seemed to enjoy it so much and I liked it too. He asked if he could touch me down there. I didn't know what to say but he moved his hand inside and stroked me all over it. Inside my stomach was rolling and rolling. I had and never have felt anything like it before or after.

Then he rubbed my bust and my nipples stood up and I was becoming breathless like he had when that white stuff appeared from his thing.
He climbed on top of me and placed his thing close to mine and started pushing up and down. I was so afraid and yet I was feeling so excited at the feeling going through my body."
"What happened then did he enter you?"
"I don't know because his brother burst in and caught us. He ran downstairs and told his mother and she came up and gave us a real talking to."
"My God how embarrassing for you what happened then did she stop you seeing each other?"
"Well in two weeks I had been sent here she told them that she had no place for me."
"Have you seen him since then?"
"No not a word."
"So you still say that you don't know if you are a virgin?"

"No what do you think?"

"Well if he didn't enter you then yes you will still be a virgin. I can't believe that you could do that though."

"I can recommend it though Helen. You are not telling me that you wouldn't feel it exciting. I tell you it is a feeling second to none. I can't imagine how good it would be if I had climaxed."

Helen even though with the drink inside could not admit that she had felt something whilst Joan was describing the incident. She had felt moisture running between her legs but didn't know what it was.

"I think that I need another drink how about you Joan?"

"No I think that I have had enough for now I think I need to go to bed."

"All right Joan I think that I have had enough and I feel tired also. I will see you in the morning. Goodnight."

"Goodnight Helen, sweet dreams."

Helen was thinking about the story that Joan had been telling her. She wondered whether she would ever get that feeling if it felt that good.

Chapter Eight

Two weeks had passed since Helen and Joan had enjoyed the bottles of wine and Joan had told Helen about her adventures with her foster brother.
She had not forgotten that conversation and had wondered if it would ever happen to her before very long.
Mrs. Freeman sent for her it was ten o'clock on Tuesday morning and Helen was hoping that Mrs. Freeman had not found out about their drinking session. Helen told Joan about the invite but Joan was not too worried that Mrs. Freeman had found out who could have told her.
Helen arrived and knocked on the office door. A voice called her in and she took a deep breath and entered.
"Good morning Helen I have some great news for you. We have managed to find the whereabouts of Mrs. Hackforth. She lives just two miles from her

believe it or not. I have made an appointment for you to see her tomorrow if you feel ready to meet her."

Helen was a little shaken but this was what she had been looking for so there was no point in being afraid.

"Thank you Mrs. Freeman I don't know what I am going to say to her at this moment in time."

"Well Helen just remember that you did nothing wrong when you left there. She loved children and I am sure you will be made very welcome."

Helen smiled and nodded her head understanding what Mrs. Freeman was telling her.

Helen left Mrs. Freeman and went to find Joan to tell her the news.

Joan gave Helen a hug she had some idea what Helen was feeling like.

"Nervous times these Helen if you like I will come with you. You never know it could help but it is up to you."

"No I think that I have to face this myself. If I remember she was kind to me even though I did not stay very long. In fact I am surprised that she remembered me. Anyway thank you for your offer Joan."

That night in bed Helen hardly slept trying to rehearse what she was going to talk to Mrs. Hackforth about. What if anything could she tells her about her life before she lived with her. As it always does the morning came and Helen felt tired after her restless night's sleep. She had breakfast and sat quiet Joan knew not to pester her at that moment.

The journey to Mrs. Hackforths seemed much longer than the two miles that Mrs. Freeman had told her. Finally arriving at the front door of the house she hesitated before setting off up the short path to the front door.

The door opened by an old looking lady. At first Helen did not recognise her. She had pictured the lady who had looked after her as a much younger woman but that was ten or more years ago. People change but she had suddenly gone grey and had seemed to have aged much more than those years.

"Hello Helen welcome. You haven't changed apart from turning into a lovely young lady."

She held out her arms to welcome Helen and suddenly the fright had left Helen's body.

She took hold of Mrs. Hackforth and cried as they hugged each other for what seemed a lifetime. Finally they went in doors and Helen felt a lot better than she had at the start of that journey.

Mrs. Hackforth offered Helen a cup of tea.

"How have you been Helen I hope that everything turned out all right for you?"

"Yes it was strange at first but the people who took me in after I left you were very kind. I stayed with them until I was sixteen and then Mr. James died and Mrs. James became ill. They had no options but to place me in Homelands but that is all right too."

"Have you seen Mrs. James did you say, since then?"

"Oh yes I visit her in the hospice most days when I can."

"Hospice why is she going to die?"

"They thought that she might they could not find anything wrong but she was slowly slipping away. I went along and tried to make her know that I was there. I played her favourite music for hours on end. She started to improve and then her lost son came home from Australia and I think that she knows but it will take time and we need to be patient."

"You are a good girl Helen, sorry a good young lady."

"How have you been then Mrs. Hackforth?"

"Please Helen, Muriel. You are a young lady now and Mrs. Hackforth sounds awful."

"Oh thank you but what…

"Oh I have been all right. We all have our problems but no one said that life was easy. I don't foster anymore now not since our Sam... oh sorry you don't know...

"Yes I remember Sam."

"No he is in prison I was heartbroken I never ever thought that any of my family would be sent to prison. I have tried to keep them on the straight and narrow all my life. I had so many plans for them but that was just a dream."

Muriel started to cry.

"It is not your fault I know has a parent you want to keep them safe but they have to take on their own responsibility. You can't live their lives for them can you? Listen to me I have no idea what it takes to be a parent. I know that we all make mistakes but some are worse than others are. What was it that Sam did that sent him to jail?"

"Drugs he became involved in drugs. Luckily he didn't take them himself but I felt so ashamed and I had to leave Darton I could not live amongst all those people that I once called friends. They painted scum on our front wall when they found out about his activities. You would know about that though wouldn't you Helen?"

Helen looked puzzled by the statement.

"Sorry Muriel I don't understand, why should I know about that?"

"Well with what happened at Mrs. Taylor's their home was daubed with paint."

"Mrs. Taylor's was it? I remember once Mr Taylor chasing some lads away and that he was real mad with them calling them vandals."

"Yes that was it. That was what I was telling you."

"Yes but he wasn't selling drugs or anything. Anyway that was why I wanted to see you. I wanted to ask you if Mr. and Mrs. Taylor were my parents."

"Why don't you know?"

"I am not sure I know my name is Taylor and I lived with them until I was six or seven in fact right up to coming to live with you. But someone told me that they fostered me and I don't understand that. If they were not my parents where did they go?"

Mrs. Hackforth looked at Helen not knowing really what she should tell her.

"Do you have any idea's Muriel? If you have please tell me I need to know I can't find any of my papers, papers like my birth certificate that could tell me something, anything that would help me trace my roots."

Muriel once again felt this quandary and was not sure what she should do. When Helen had come to her it was said by the social people that her identity had to be kept secret, but that was twelve years ago. Helen was now an adult and she ought to know about her background.

"What if I was to put you in touch with the Taylor's Helen would that help?"

"You mean that they are still living around here?"

"No not around here but I still met them at the foster agents in Barnsley for a while. Then I had to move so I haven't seen then since that time. That must be around twelve months ago now. I could get in touch with the agency and try and find where they are living now."

"Were they still living in Birdwell when you met them last?"

"Oh no they left there just after you came to live with me. Something happened and they had to move quite quickly I understand."

"Why had they done something wrong they were such kind people, no I can't see that they would do anything wrong."

"No I don't think that they did Helen. It was something else but I am not sure what it was.

Perhaps they will tell you when you meet them again."

"Do you think that they would want to meet me again? It was not because of me that they had to move was it?"

"Of course not you were a lovely little girl why would you think that you silly girl?"

Helen felt a ting of sadness for a moment.

"When do you think we could find out Muriel?"

"I will give the agency a ring right now and see if they can help. It may be a different matter trying to get hold of the Taylor's though, still we can only try. Here I will get you another cup of tea whilst I telephone the agency."

The telephone was outside the room in the hall near to the front door. Muriel brought in Helen's second cup of tea and then left the room closing the door behind her.

Helen shuffled along the couch trying to hear what was going on out there on the telephone. She felt nervous more nervous than when she came to see Muriel. The Taylor's had looked after her for a lot longer than Muriel and had never tried to get in touch with her since they moved her out of their home. Did she do something that was so terrible that that nice couple could just be shut of her like some old shoe?

Muriel seemed to be ages on the telephone and Helen could just hear an occasional word from Muriel but didn't know what that word meant in context with whom she was talking to. It was so frustrating. Finally Helen heard the small ring that told her that the telephone had been replaced on the receiver. She shuffled back along the couch to where she had been sitting when Muriel had left the room. She looked at Muriel in anticipation of what she might be told.

Muriel sat down and Helen turned her body so that they were face to face.

"Well did they know?"

Muriel hesitated. "Yes they know they had moved, twice to be exact they do not foster anymore but the agency still have them on their books."

Helen waited with her mouth half open, just waiting to hear where they lived and would they see her.

"Is it far from here?"

"If I told you I don't think that you would believe me. Because I didn't believe what they were telling me when they told me, if that makes sense."

"Yes it makes sense. What was it that you did not believe Muriel?"

"They finally moved to Darton and they live next door to where I lived can you believe that Helen. Your first foster parents lived next door to where your second foster parents, that is me, lived I find that just uncanny don't you?"

Helen wasn't too bothered that they had moved close to where she once lived but what was more important was that they still were alive.

"When can I go and see them Muriel?"

"Now there is a thing that I can't answer not right at this moment. They are going to get in touch with them and ask them if they would be willing to see you. They do know the background but they wouldn't tell me what it was so I still can't help you there."

Muriel crossed her fingers behind her back. She did know the reason and had all the time but she could not tell Helen. The job of telling Helen would be the responsibility of someone more qualified than she was.

"Anyway they are going to keep in touch with me and if I hear something I will telephone you at the home. I do hope that they are willing to see you Helen."

"I do also Muriel you know I was so happy living with them, not that I was not happy when I lived with you. The shock of just being moved will live with me forever."

"Yes I knew that you were upset and had difficulty settling here with me. However I knew that I could not have you for long and that did not give me a lot of time to get to know you like I should. I can only apologise for that Helen."

Muriel leaned over and kissed Helen on the cheek. "You have had enough to worry about Muriel with Sam. You did nothing wrong you are a good mother but we kids are our own worst enemies you know. We never listen and always know what is best for us."

"You are a good girl Helen and I wish that I had known you for longer. We could have become really good friends I know that for a fact. I can tell immediately if I will like the person that comes to live here with me."

"That is very nice of you to say that Muriel. What happened to Mr. Hackforth I never met him whilst I lived with you did I?"

"No love you didn't I'm afraid that Mr. Hackforth, Tom, a lovely man, he was killed in a mining accident about three years before you came to live with me. We had always fostered and I could not see why I should stop when I lost Tom. Besides it helped me through that sorry time."

Muriel went quiet for a while as her thoughts sprung back to those terrible days.

"You know you never feel that you will get over tragedies in your life like that but God gives you strength and you do somehow."

"That is why I feel that I must find out about myself. I feel like something inside me has died and I don't know what it is. There is something missing that I know I need to find out. I suppose it is like the grieving process even though I don't know what that feels like."

If anything had not made Muriel determined to help Helen her last statement had. If she felt inside like she had when she lost her Tom then she is feeling bad. At eighteen she should not be allowed to feel like that. No she has to know.

"Excuse me Helen once again whilst I make a phone call."

Off she went again out into the hallway but this time she left the door open.

Helen heard her talking to someone and this time her voice had more aggression without being offensive.

"Yes and I need to know today in the next hour if that could be possible. You are most generous, thank you."

Muriel returned the phone on to the receiver.

"Helen I think that I will make us a fresh cup of tea. I don't want you to leave just yet I have something to show you and I am waiting for the agency to ring me back. So make yourself comfortable we are going to try and solve your problem today or my name is not Muriel Hackforth."

Helen was not sure why this sudden aggressive mannerism had taken over Muriel. The fact that she was showing so much determination to help her gave Helen more hope that she could discover her roots. She was not sure when she first arrived at Mrs. Hackforth's in fact just the opposite. There seemed to be something, a barrier that Muriel had erected between them and she didn't understand why that should be.

Surely it can't be that hard to understand that everyone needed to know who they were and where they belonged. This was a simple civil liberty the basis of civilisation.

Helen spent the next two hours talking about her life after the Hackforth's and how she had met Joan and Andrew. The fact that another foster parent had left her without knowing why but now she had began to understand. She had learned that it was not her fault and that she had been loved and that had made a significant difference to her.

"Will Mrs. James recover then Helen?"

"We, well the doctors are pretty sure she will but there could be complications with her mental side. I am going to help as much as I possibly can. She looked after me when I needed it and I will not desert her when she needs help."

After a while the telephone rang and Muriel half ran to answer it.

"Yes I understand well I will get in touch with them. They could come here and talk. Yes I will do that and thank you very much."

Helen wanted to ask Muriel what she was talking about but Muriel had pushed the buttons on the phone and listened for someone to lift the receiver at the other end.

"Hello Muriel Hackforth here. Yes it has been a long time I hope that you and Mr. Taylor, Bill, isn't it? Yes, me too. Well I just wanted to see if you would come here to my house and see Helen. I have her here with me today. Yes she does deserve

that. Well I would like to see you we have so much in common you could come to lunch if you like. Tomorrow would be fine; shall I arrange it then? Right then I will do that. It is so nice to hear your voice again Betty I can't believe that it has been so long since we last talked. How can we be like that, friends need to keep in touch whether they move or not? I will expect you tomorrow then around eleven. See you tomorrow then and thank you."
Helen sat up straight her nerves were really on edge at what she had heard. It was finally happening she asked herself if she was ready for it.
"The Taylor's are coming over tomorrow Helen. Can you be here for lunch say about eleven o'clock? They are still concerned that someone may recognise and it could start all over again."
"Recognise, recognise what Muriel?"
"They will explain tomorrow Helen. Sleep on it tonight and tomorrow it will all be straightened out."

"Sleep on what? How can I sleep on something that I have no idea as to what it is?"

Muriel felt trapped.

"I am so sorry that I can't tell you anymore. I can't make you understand because I do not know sufficient about it so please be patient with me Helen."

"Yes Muriel you're right but I know that you understand how I am feeling at this moment."

"Yes I do but let's wait until tomorrow. You know I am impatient to know of your story Helen. Come on drink up and give yourself time to absorb what it is that you are going to learn tomorrow."

Helen drank up and said her goodbyes to Mrs. Hackforth. They kissed each other and Helen felt that she had been visiting Muriel for a long time not that she had seen Muriel for some ten years or so, life is so funny.

Helen made her way back to Homelands keen to let Joan know about her visit. She felt strange and emotional at the thought of what tomorrow may bring.

Mrs. Freeman was placing some new notices on the board when Helen walked into the house. They smiled at each other.

"Is it good news then Helen? Are you any wiser for your efforts?"

"A mixture of emotions but it is true that I do feel better. The fact that I met Mrs. Hackforth again was great she is a lovely woman and considering what she has gone through she is amazing. She managed to arrange a meeting with the Taylor's for me tomorrow."

"How do you feel about that then?"

"Excited and yet scared to death about it. The thought that I could find that…

"Find out what? What is it that you think you will find out that could be so frightening?"

"I don't know Mrs. Freeman that is what worries me, I just don't know."

"Then why put yourself through this?"

"I have to know Mrs. Freeman. I just have to know you can understand that, can't you. You don't feel that I am being silly do you?"

"No I don't Helen. In your position I would do exactly what you are doing. You just have to settle yourself otherwise the stress could make you ill. Go on go to your room and have a rest before tea. I know that when I feel like you do I go and have a lie down for a minute or two. You know you girls can stress us out you know. Of course I wouldn't want you to tell any of the girls we are supposed to be professionals aren't we."

They both laughed and Helen left Mrs. Freeman still replacing notices on the board.

Back at Mrs. Hackforth's she had sorted some old photographs out and spread them out on the table in front of her. She was looking for one in particular it was one taken early in her and Tom's marriage. It had a special place in her heart and she often talked to it when she felt down and depressed.

She knew that it was in this particular box of photo's and soon had it I her grasp.

Looking down at what today looked like an old fashioned photograph and the two people in it were so young. Muriel smiled as she spoke to the man in the picture.

"Tom, my Tom, we were so young. I still can feel your hand in mine even though so many years have passed since we held our hands together. I have a problem Tom I know that I always seem to burden you with my problems, but you were always so good at solving my problems. You didn't meet Helen when she lived with me but I know that you would have loved her like one of your own. She was a young girl with problems that no young girl should have. She was born at the wrong time and in the wrong time.

Tomorrow this lovely girl, now that is right she is now a lovely young woman. Well tomorrow she has to come face to face with what could be her own personal nightmare. It was not of her making but the cards have fallen her way.

I know that when you were living through that strike in 1984 you had no time for those who worked whilst others fought for what they believed was the future of their industry and the future prospects of their sons. Well some didn't have that choice because they were just babies at the time. The children including our own had to suffer without having the knowledge as to why their parents and especially the father's were fighting in the streets. Why did they have no food only what people handed out to them?

Well this young woman is going to wonder why it was that the friends and neighbours and even members of her own family drove her father to suicide.

I do not know how she is going to react when she hears that. I keep thinking how I would feel in her position but there is no way of knowing."

Muriel looked down at the photograph.

"I do wish that you could tell me what to do. How can I prepare myself to help Helen? There are so many secrets that Helen has to discover before she knows about her life. I think that she is strong but she will need to be to take in what is facing her tomorrow."

Muriel leaned over and kissed the face of Tom. Tears rolled down her face but she knew that he helped her in the past and he would not fail her now.

Chapter Nine

The following morning which to Helen had seemed like a lifetime in coming Joan was sat at the table waiting for Helen to appear.

"How did you go on yesterday I looked for you?"
"Fine it turned out better than I could have hoped. In fact I am meeting the Taylor's at lunch time today."
"The Taylor's how on earth did you find them?"
"Mrs. Hackforth knew something and she asked the agency for the address. No that is correct she insisted that they tell her and contact the Taylor's for me. She was marvellous Joan absolutely marvellous. I don't think that I would have found them because they had moved since I lived with them. There is something strange about the move but anyway Muriel...
"Muriel. Who is Muriel?"

"Mrs. Hackforth. Well she found out that they had moved from the agency and you will never guess where they had moved to."

"No go on where to?"

Only the next door to where I lived when I was with the Hackforth's."

"But you told me that Mrs. Freeman told you that the Hackforth's had moved from the address where you lived."

"Yes they did but the Taylor's moved in next door to where they lived when they lived there."

Joan shook her head in amazement.

"That is unbelievable what did Mrs. Hackforth or Muriel say to that?"

"She was like us, amazed."

"Could I come with you?"

Helen would have dearly loved to say yes, but she knew that she couldn't.

"I am sorry Joan but you know that I can't say yes. A lot of what I am doing I am not sure whether it is legal or not. I do know that the Taylor's will be feeling as fearful as I am at this moment. We have not seen other for all those years and we don't know anything about each other at this moment. Yes they know more about me than I do about them but they still have to tell me and meet me after all those years when they gave me up without any explanation."

"I can understand what you are saying Helen and I respect that I didn't want to seem to be pushing myself on you."

"I know that Joan and you have no idea how much I appreciate your offer but I am not sure how the Taylor's will react because they do seem to have tried to avoid our meeting for all these years. I have no doubt they had their reasons but I have a problem in knowing why that should be. They would take foster children in because they cared for children so why did they appear to change. You know I always thought that they were my parents until Mrs. Hackforth told me that they were not."

Joan looked shocked. "You mean that they are not your parents?"

"No it seems they fostered me from being a baby. I had a feeling about this though from speaking to Mrs. James when she was well but I never really understood. It seems to have been a coincidence that we had the same surname."

"That was some coincidence that Helen. How did you feel when Mrs. Hackforth told you?"

"Like you, shocked. I had wanted to think that once I found the Taylor's I would have found my parents. Obviously that is not going to be the case however they must know my parents if they took me in as a baby, don't you think Joan?"

"I would think so, strange isn't it. I never had that problem so I can't imagine what sort of nightmare it must be for you."

"Well I am going to take all the papers and photographs that I have just in case they could help. As yet I have not solved the mystery of my birth certificate someone must have it. Anyway the Taylor's should have some ideas as to where it may be surely. That should tell me then who my mother and father are."

"All I can wish you is the best of luck if anyone deserves to know you do Helen."

"Thank you Joan I don't think that I would have had the strength to get this far without your support. Anything that I find out will be in some way thanks to you and I will never forget that." Helen took hold of Joan and gave her a love and a kiss on her cheek.

"Do you mind if I leave you now Joan. I need to go through those papers and get ready for that very important lunch at Muriel. I will let you know how I get on when I come back whatever time it is."

Mrs. Hackforth was busy preparing a small but a little special lunch. She had bought lots of nibbles for the starter and a ham salad for main. The salad should be safe just in case people were vegetarians or not. They could have fish or fresh cut golden ham. A cheesecake would finish off with a selection of cheeses.

Not knowing who drank she decided that she would buy in a couple of bottles of red and white wine. They could also have tea or coffee if required. She felt rather nervous about it all even though she was not a woman that normally suffered with her nerves. She had organised much bigger lunches before and had felt no nerves at all. This was different however she had invited two lots of people that had their own needs as to what they took away from this meeting.

She cleaned up for the fifth time that day again pure nerves but she knew that once they arrived she would be all right.

The hands on the clock seemed to be moving very slowly but they were going up to the time when the Taylor's would arrive. Mrs. Hackforth had arranged that they should arrive a little earlier than Helen to enable them to have a short discussion about the meeting should. Now that Mrs. Hackforth had met Helen she had a better understanding of what she wanted to know. Not just wanted but determined to find out whatever the cost. Before they faced Helen the Taylor's would need to know how she was feeling.

The Taylor's arrived on time, which was a great relief for Muriel. She greeted them and invited them into the lounge and asked if they would like a cup of tea. They declined the offer but congratulated her on her home. They asked if she was expecting company when they saw the food laid out under cover so as to keep any flying insects from enjoying it before they had chance to eat it.

"No it is for us when we are ready. I thought that we may talk for some time and get a little peckish." Mr. Taylor smiled. "I will need to be a little more than peckish Muriel."

"Well how are you both keeping these days? I haven't apart from the occasional phone call seen you since I left Darton. I tell you what you could have knocked me down with a feather when they told me where you are now living. You do realise that I lived next door don't you?"

"Next door, no I didn't, I knew that you lived in Darton but not next door that is so strange?"

"Well Betty and John we have a little problem that I feel we need to face. I have met Helen and she has made a lovely young woman. She thought that you were her parents and was a little shocked when I told her that you were not he4r actual parents. I had to tell her because she felt so let down that if you were her parents as to the reason that you had never tried to make contact with her over all those years."

"You know why Muriel so why didn't you tell her?"

"I almost did but then I felt that we needed to tell her together because if she didn't talk to you I believe that she would still have wondered. The facts have to be faced by all of us. I feel that whatever we do Helen is still going to be hurt but I hope that she will understand."

"Why is it that this has to come out now? I thought that we had covered the tracks so well."

"I told you Betty, this is a very intelligent young woman and although we have all been a small part of her life we should take some credit for that. That is why she deserves to know why we took her in and more importantly why we had to let her go."

John nodded his head. "Muriel's right Betty place yourself in her position what would you need to do?"

"I know that Muriel's right John I don't need you to tell me that. I am just thinking of what we all had to take whilst she was with us it was not easy you know. Perhaps the last sixteen years have clouded the judgement. You know what they did to us…Do we want that to start all over again?"

"I am not sure that it will start again there has a lot of water has passed under the bridge since those dark days."

"What do you think Muriel do you think that it is all forgotten?"

"No I don't I don't think that it ever will be. It is now a part of history and will always be remembered whenever the media talk about Maggie Thatcher and her fight with the unions. However we have to remember that Helen was born three months after the strike started how can any reasonable human being say that any of it was her fault? There was a complete new generation born in that period are they all going to be held responsible for what the adults did then?"

The three of them became quiet. Muriel looked up at the clock.

"Helen will be anytime now. I will put the kettle on ready so that we can have lunch and then…well we will see where we go after that. I do hope that we can be honest if nothing else. We have to think of Helen and not of ourselves otherwise this will never ever go away."

Helen finally arrived inside she was shivering as the apprehensive fear started to take over. She knew that if she was to learn something this afternoon she must take control of herself. She stopped and took deep breaths something she had learned from her earlier yoga classes. Placing her hands on her stomach she breathed in and out and searched for that place where she knew she would be calm. It slowly began to work and she felt more in control. The front door of Mrs. Hackforth's opened and the welcome was there. Helen knew that whatever happened Muriel would be by her side, a friend whom she had only met yesterday again after all those years but felt that she had known her all of her life.

"Come in Helen, Betty and John Taylor are here already."

"I'm not late am I?"

"No of course not come in and meet them. I bet you are feeling a little nervous just like me aren't you?"

"I am a little nervous."

"Well don't they are lovely I don't know how much you remember about them but we will soon put that right."

Muriel took Helen into the lounge and John Taylor stood up when they entered the room.

"Helen this is Betty Taylor and her husband John. Betty and John this is Helen Taylor."

They all nervously shook hands.

"I am so pleased to meet you once again Helen. Muriel told us that you had grown into a lovely young woman and I agree with her."

"Thank you Mrs. Taylor that is very kind of you to say. I don't think I am but…

"Nonsense you are beautiful."

Helen felt her face start to blush at the attention she was receiving and Muriel knew exactly how she was feeling.

"Now then how about that cup of tea I think that we could all do with one by now I know that I could."

"That would be very nice Muriel."

"Right I will leave you three just for a moment if you want something to eat feel free to help yourself from the table."

"I will come and help you Muriel."

"No honestly Helen it is all right. I am sure that you and Betty and John have much to talk about."

Muriel left the room and the silence could have been cut with a knife. Finally it was John that spoke first.

"Well Helen and what do you do. Muriel tells us you are staying at a place called Homelands in Doncaster."

"I work in the main library."

"That sounds interesting what is it that you do there?"

"I work with the students finding what the needs are and matching our intake so that they can always get hold of the reference books they will all need. It is very interesting work and I enjoy it very much."

"What about Homelands do they take good care of you there?"

"Oh yes it is a lovely homely place. Mrs. Freeman is very good in fact it was she that started this road that I am now walking. Trying to find out who I am is so important to me. I have felt something is missing and it doesn't help moving forward if you are not sure from where you came. I hope that you can understand that."

"Yes Helen we can. Muriel, Mrs. Hackforth explained to us a little of what you know about your background."

"Not very much I'm afraid."

"No she told us that you believed that we were your parents for a long time."

"Yes I did but I know now that our having the same name is just coincidence."

Betty and John looked at each other. This was the first thing that needed correcting.

"Well that is not quite true Helen. We changed your name to ours....

"You changed it whatever did you do that for?"

Again they looked at each other.

"We had to for your sake Helen."

Helen could not help but look them both in the eyes.

"Is Helen my true name then?"

"No not really it was Mary...."

"Mary. Who gave you the right to change it then?"

"This is very difficult for us Helen. I know that at this moment you will find it hard to believe that whatever happened was for your own benefit."

"My benefit, how do you make that out? You have just told me that my name is not Helen it is Mary and that my last name is not Taylor... so what is it?"

"I am not sure that we ought to say not just yet. I think that we need to explain how you came to be with us and then the reason for changing your name will be much clearer."

Mrs. Hackforth came in with a teapot and a tray of cups.

"Now then you three have you been getting to know one another whilst I was making the tea?"

Helen looked at her.

"Getting to know one another, yes you could say that Muriel. I now learn that not only has my life been a lie even my name is not right. I'm not called Helen my name is Mary and I am not called Taylor but as yet I have no idea as to what my surname is. Yes you could say that we are finding out about one another."

"I am so sorry Helen I didn't mean that you found out like this. I am sure that Betty and John here only wish to give you all the facts that you need to make sense of all this. Just show a little patience and all will become clear. Take my word for it Helen I am not here to create more sadness in your life. Can you believe me?"

Helen took more deep breaths.

"Yes I can and I am so sorry for my outburst. I have felt so tight about this meeting that it was not easy to take in. I know that you must have had good reasons to do what you did. Again I am so sorry."

"That is all right Helen. I would feel very much like you. I could have handled that a bit better but you asked me a direct question of which only the truth could be replied. I have no idea how I could have answered it in any other way."

Helen shook her head in agreement.

"Right let's have this cup of tea then we can all feel a little better. I feel that now that we have got that out of the way we will all get on a lot better for it. We are here for one common reason and that must be remembered."

Everyone took a cup and Muriel poured out the tea.

"Sandwich or nibble anyone. There are loads and it all has to be eaten before we finish here. I am on a diet and it will only get wasted if you don't eat it."

"You on a diet Muriel there is not enough of you as it is. You don't need to lose weight you look well and healthy."

"Thank you John."

"He never pays me compliments like that Muriel."

"What I remember of John Betty, he always pays you many a compliment. My Tom used to laugh when I told him that he should show me that sort of respect."

"Yes we heard about the loss of Tom he was such a good and kind man Muriel. I bet you still miss those practical jokes he played all the time."

"Yes it is not easy when you lose someone but.... Muriel took hold of Helen. "But it is harder when you can't remember or are unaware of who your loved ones were, like Helen here and that is why it is important that we do our best to help her."

Helen felt a lot better maybe it was the tea but inside she felt calm and settled. She was now beginning to believe that here were three people that could help her understand her life for once.

"Yes Helen we did make life difficult for you, didn't we? I suppose that if we look back in hindsight we were a little cowardly about the whole thing…

"That is nonsense and you know that Betty I know for a fact that you did what you could and absorbed so much trouble. No you have nothing to blame yourself for between the government and the union leaders well that didn't help. We all suffered and the children most of all. They had no say in what was happening and I don't think that Maggie considered that in her plan."

"I do not suppose that she did but what about Scargill? I think that they were both as bad. Compromise became something that neither could accept from each other."

"Well we all now know what it led up to. Look at the devastation that has hit us all. Looking back those communities enjoyed so much together. Remember the street parties and how we all looked after one another. All lost and for what?"

"Did my father work in the mines then Mrs. Taylor?"

Muriel's mind swung back to Helen with her question.

"Yes he did love he went down the mines when he was fifteen. He used to work with his father, your grandfather. They were good workers in fact all the families did their bit. Working down the pit was not an easy job many a man had been injured over the years and some were killed. God bless them." Betty remembered Tom. "Sorry Muriel for bringing back those memories."

"Not to worry Betty I have got over that now life must move on. Tom is very much in my heart, never forgotten but you can't live your life around the past. I know that we have been saying about the lost communities but like Tom that is the past and we need to move on from there."

Helen was beginning to feel that the troubles caused by the miners' strike had some bearing on her past but at that moment she was not too clear on how.

"Did my father get killed down the pit then?"

"No love not exactly. I think that it would be true to say that the pit helped to kill him."

"How did he die then if he wasn't killed down the pit how did he die?"

Muriel took hold of Helen she knew that what Betty was about to say would be hard to understand by someone who didn't really know her father.

"I'm afraid that he killed himself Helen. It was a shock to everyone who knew him. He was such a kind caring man. He loved his music…

"He loved music you say?"

"Oh yes he played in the village brass band for years. He started as a junior and played right through the ranks up to the seniors."

"What instrument did he play then?"

"Trumpet I think I am not converse with all the instruments but I think it was the trumpet. Most of those that played had skills with many instruments within the band."

"When did he die then?"

"1986. There was snow on the ground when they found him."

"Found him why where was he?"

"In the wood close to the village, behind where he had practised with the brass band for many years in fact it was a band member that found him."

"He was all alone out there why? How could a man who was so kind and caring finish all alone out there on that cold day?"

No one had the answer to Helen's question. They and a lot more people had asked themselves that question over the years.

"Why did he have to take his own life what was so bad? Did he and my mother have problems? Did he do it because I had been born?"

"No none of those and especially not because you were born. He was so proud of his first born. He was a big man but he could be seen pushing you around in your pram around the village."

"There had to be a reason no one ends a happy life. I just don't understand. What did my mother do when she was told?"

"Devastated that was the only way anyone could describe her feelings."

The tears started to roll down the women's faces as they came to terms with the thoughts of that time.

"Did they find out why he did it? I mean that was eight years ago surely the police found the reason behind his death."

Muriel and Betty both looked at each other and Helen caught sight of the glance.

"What is it? What is it that you are not telling me?"

"It was the strike love. It was the strike that caused your father's death."

"The strike how did the strike cause his death?"

Helen could feel that this was causing a great deal of pain and difficulty trying to tell her. She knew that somewhere inside they were trying to not hurt her feelings about what they had to say. This was always going to be an emotional time for everyone. "Well you had just been born months after the miners' strike took hold. The miners felt that they would only be out there for a matter of weeks. The confidence was very high after the last confrontation with the Heath Government but it soon became obvious that this was going to be different. Now miners didn't have a lot of money behind them they were not the ones for piling money into savings and things like that enough to put a roof over the heads of their families and food on the table and perhaps a week or two weeks at Cleethorpes in a caravan. They could not afford for this strike to last too long otherwise the money for bills like rent, electricity and food would soon begin to diminish and fast.

Some families found it harder than others did and after weeks and weeks without wages coming in some found survival impossible.

Your father could see that your mother was finding life very difficult but she never grumbled but tried her best to bring you up and find food for the family. Some of the shops especially those in the villages tried to help by allowing people to build up bills on credit but they soon began to find it difficult as the strike went on and on.

Soon your father like many others decided that they had a decision to make not an easy decision but it had to be made. They knew that their friends and work colleagues would have difficulty in understanding their motives and would probably see them as deserters and cowards.

Your father was very brave and walked off to the pit with others from the village. When the rest of the village found out they stood chanting at them and throwing stones and grass sods as they walked the streets. Finally the police had to offer protection to them all and started to bus them into work. The buses were pelted with eggs and stones and the village was filled with so much aggression. That aggression soon started to not just attack the buses but the homes of those who had taken the decision to return to work.

They threw bricks and stones at the windows of the homes and painted 'Scab' all over the walls of the homes. The police tried to give some protection but that was impossible twenty-four hours a day.

The young men who had no family became what they saw as vigilantes determined to protect those that were out on strike. Even the men's own families turned on them and that turned the tide for a lot of the men who had decided to break the strike.

That was the last straw it was felt for your father. His father, your grandfather was a strong member of the union and he made the choice after trying to change your father's mind. He failed and so he turned his back on him and would not allow your grandmother your father's mother to talk to him. Can you imagine how your father must have felt when that happened? He was only trying to save his own family and yet those he should have been able to rely on just turned their backs on him when he needed them the most."

Helen was shocked by what she was hearing and could not find any words to reply or ask questions. She sat there and felt that someone was telling her a story not a true story but a fictional nightmare of a story.

"Are you all right Helen? What about another cup of tea?"

Helen shook her head.

"Would you like us to go on Helen if you are finding it too much we could always stop and see you another time when you have had time to take some of this in. It can't be easy for you."

Helen pulled herself together. There was no way that she could afford to allow these people to move away with this still untold.

"No please carry on it does not matter when we face this it will just be as hard."

"You were about six months old and your mother was desperate she had lost her husband and the life insurance refused to pay her any of the money that was due on the death of your father.

She had no one to turn to her parents were both dead and her in-laws would have nothing to do with her and you their grandchild. That must have been so hard for your mother don't you think?"

Again all that Helen could do was to shake her head as the story unfolded.

"How on earth did she?

"Well she looked to others for help but none came. It would seem that anyone that wanted to help received letters and threats from anonymous sources. Now, we should ask ourselves where was that community spirit that had pulled us through the war years this was untrue and no one deserved that sort of treatment from any source.

Then six months later your grandfather was found hanging from the same tree as your father was. There seemed at the time to be no suspicious circumstances but then the police began to think that maybe someone had found out that your grandfather had tried to help your mother secretly."

"Had he? Had he really tried to help mother?"

"No one knew at the time and no one was charged with the death of your grandfather. Your grandmother started getting threats and someone threw a brick through her window and it hit her on the head. She finished in hospital and that is when things started to change.

You see your grandmother had been the centrepiece of the village. She had brought into the world most of the children. When it was found out that someone had done this to her everyone demanded that whoever had done it should be handed to the police. It was not long before the culprit had been found. Not a young boy, not youths roaming the streets looking for trouble, but a family man he should have known better. The police about the death of your grandfather questioned him but they could not prove anything. They did however prove that he had thrown the brick through the window and had hurt your grandmother so he was sent to prison for one month. That was not the worst thing that happened to him though the community turned him and his family out of the village themselves."

"Good so they should have. How did my grandmother recover?"

After a while she recovered but she was not the same woman that we all knew. She became reserved and stopped taking part in whatever was going on. The villages tried to take care of her but she declined their offers."

"What happened to my mother then?"

"We didn't know, no one did she just disappeared from the village whilst the attention was focused on your grandmother. Then something strange happened a child was found on the steps of the Mineworkers Union Headquarters in Barnsley, locally known as King Arthur's Castle, yes the steps of the offices of Arthur Scargill. She blamed him for placing her and you in this position. She knew that there would be no way in which she could look after you like a child deserved. The people one-time friends and neighbours had driven her away. We were all to blame for allowing these things to happen."

"Hold on Betty you were not to blame you didn't live in the village so you had nothing to do with it. So don't you go blaming yourself, Helen would not be here if it had not been for you and John."

Helen looked at Muriel seeking out what she meant by that statement.

"Betty and John heard about this child that had been found on the steps of the offices through the hospital. Betty here spent a lot of her time hospital visiting those who had no one or whose family didn't want to know.

They contacted the social services, which knew them for the work that they did with other children. They had some clues as to the identity because your mother had placed a birth certificate inside the blanket and a short letter stating why she had done this. The police tried to find your mother but she had disappeared and it was feared that she might have done herself some harm like your father. They thought that she was just another victim of the miner's strike.

Anyway Betty and John were approached to see if they would foster this child, you Helen, until they could find your mother. They agreed and gave you a home for the next four years or so."

"Why did they let you go?"

Helen turned to the Taylor's.

"Then why did you let me go? Didn't you love me?"

"Of course we did but things started to become very difficult. We changed your name as recommended by the police and social services and kept your birth certificate in hiding."

"Why?"

"There were still some people out there who were after the families of the 'Scabs' would you believe that they still are at this moment in time. The depth of that strike was so deep that it has sunk through generations. They still believe that they could have won that war if the 'Scabs' had not broken the strike. We all know that this was the biggest mistake they could have made. No one was bigger than the country and they were doomed the day they took action."

"But what had that got to do with me?"

"They started using us to try and get to you and your mother. They had a strong belief that we knew where your mother was hiding. They started scrolling bad words on the walls of our home and accusing us of all sorts of nasty things. We could not go to the shops without being accosted by youths in hoods to cover their faces. Things were getting rather nasty and it was then that we realised what your parents must have gone through.

We contacted social services and in the middle of the night they smuggled you over to Darton to Mrs. Hackforth's, Muriel here. We could not contact you because it was important that no one knew where you had gone. They still played us up but we stuck it out and we felt that we had overcome the problem. Then things started to happen, our car was covered in paint and windows smashed when we were out. We informed the police but they could not catch them they were very clever. It was decided that we had to move like you had to so we did it without telling anyone around three years ago."

"Why didn't you contact me then when you had moved?"

"I know it sounds hard now but we had to think of you and Mrs. Hackforth. I did ask Muriel here when we met at the agency but it was like working in the secret service. Then you moved again when things quietened down. We all knew that the move to Mrs. Hackforth's could only be temporary because of her children."

"I remember Mr. Taylor chasing people away from the house. You told me they were vandals but I knew that a lot of people used to bully me when I was at school."

"Yes they did and couldn't tell you why because then you would have known about your mother and father. That was not good for an older girl never mind one of your age."

"But I am eighteen years of age now and I think that someone should have contacted me earlier than this."

"I don't think that any of us would deny that but I think that we were all ashamed of the actions of the community and also afraid to face you. Can you understand that Helen, I do hope that you can because we were only thinking of you I am sorry if you feel that we let you down."

Helen felt the genuineness in what Mrs. Taylor was saying. She knew that inside she didn't blame anyone because she didn't know whom to blame. The stories that she was now hearing were new and it had suddenly given her someone to blame but as yet she was not sure who that was.

"I do understand but it is difficult for me to grasp how people could change so much and become so evil that they drove people like my father to commit suicide like he did."

"I know love but these were desperate times. The people could not touch Maggie Thatcher and her Government and so they hit out at anything that seemed to support her regime. Unfortunately your father and the others that went into work were seen as their enemy and the friends of the Thatcher Government. We know that is not what they were they were desperate men looking to the welfare of their families. Those that stuck it out though also believed this but for different reasons. We all need to try and understand the actions of the others but I don't see that in our lifetime. Perhaps your generation can go some way to try and forgive but only time will tell."

Muriel suggested that they should have a break at that point and have some lunch.

"I don't know about you but all this talk has made me a little peckish."

No one spoke she knew that the thoughts they were all having at that moment would not be on food. She ignored the silence and handed the plates to each one and told them to help themselves while she made another pot of tea. She slipped away into the kitchen but listened for any movement from her guests. Gradually one by one they went over to the table and placed the food on to the plates provided. Muriel returned into the lounge and gave a smile to each one of her guests.

"Good for you I didn't like the fact that I may have to eat all this lot myself."

"It's lovely Muriel you have done us proud. You must let us give you something towards the cost you can't afford to pay for all this."

"Stuff and nonsense I will hear no more about that. I have one thing in mind and that is to bring all those that have been part of Helen's life together so that she has a better understanding and no go around blaming herself. I know that she must feel that no one wanted or loved her but that as we all know is totally untrue."

"Thank you Muriel I could not have said that better if I had said it myself. We did and still do love you very much Helen. I don't think there had been a day that John and I hadn't wondered how you were getting on. I know that may sound just talk, but we have to think about you and we didn't know who was watching us. I know that it sounds like a spy thriller but that is how it felt in those early years.

I can't tell you how pleased we were when we knew that you wanted to see us."

"I have wanted to contact you for sometime but I didn't think that you would see me. I thought that I had done something awful and everyone had.....

Muriel and Betty both jumped from the chairs and moved over to Helen.

"That is stuff and nonsense we loved, we all loved you very much. If it had not been for the trouble we would have loved to keep you for our own."

"Hold on Betty then I would not have had the pleasure of Helen's company. You see Helen here we are now fighting over you."

They all laughed and John took his plate over to the table and refilled it with some more food. The atmosphere was changing and everyone could feel it. They became more relaxed with each other and the food soon started to disappear from the table.

"Could I ask what happened to my mother during all of this?"

Muriel and Betty looked to each other suggesting that there was something to hide.

"Have I asked the wrong question?"

"No Helen we were just wondering who should tell you not that we have anything to hide. Go on Muriel you explain you had more dealings with it than we did."

Muriel took a deep intake of breath before she started.

"Well Helen you have to understand that we did not know your mother. We had never met her that may sound strange that we took in the child of someone that we had never met. That was fostering and this was not unusual, not at all. We often had children whose mother had perhaps gone into hospital and the father had to go to work. The social services would bring the child or children along to us and we took care of their needs until they could return home to their parents.

You were different and we knew that. Betty here had the worst job of all and that was to take in an abandoned child of whom no one really knew a great deal about. There was some information that your mother had left inside the blanket that she had carefully wrapped you in. It was obvious to the social services that whoever your mother was she had loved you very much. No one knows what it is that can turn a loving caring mother or person to do some of the things that they do. No one blamed your mother not they knew that you were the most important thing at that moment. Then when they had settled you in with a caring family then they would try and help the mother of this child. They, as I said, knew that she was not being evil when she left you. She had made sure that you were fed and warm and in a safe place where you would be found.

The police were involved because your mother became a missing person. They knew from some of the paperwork that your mother had left inside your blanket that her husband had committed suicide and that she could not give the care that a small child needed. They thought that, no they actually feared the worse and started to drag reservoirs and canals around the area. After three weeks of this type of searching they had to call off the enormous number of policemen involved in the search. They scaled it down but they never gave up.

The papers became involved when your grandmother came forward with a photograph that they could circulate in the papers both local and national.

It was six months before they heard from someone who had or they thought that they had seen her in Bradford."

"Bradford but why would she go to Bradford?"

"No one knew or no one would say. The fact that your grandmother had given the photograph to the police had caused her a great deal of problems from your grandfather. He had told her that she was not part of the family and that as far as he was concerned no one knew her."

"How did you find out about this then?"

"The police told John and me, they were very good keeping us informed about everything that was happening. You seemed to have settled with us and

we were so enjoying having you. We had always
wanted a child you know but I was unable to have
any. God had sent you to us but he had also taken
your mother away from you. These were mixed
blessings for all of us but we had one mission in life
at that time and that was you Helen. When it
became obvious that the relationship within the
family was not what it should be that is when the
social services told us that we should change your
name temporary so that you and we would have
some protection.

The feelings at that time were bad and like I said
about your grandfather and grandmother each
family as well as the communities were being
swallowed up in this deep resentment and anger of
that strike.

You were having your forth birthday when we had
the first real news about your mother. Apparently
she had been in Bradford and had stayed with
some distant relatives for a short time and then

found God. She entered some sort of religious group who cared for homeless and lost women. They had contacted the police to tell them that she was with them but had no recollection of any child. They only discovered that she was being hunted for when someone inadvertently left a newspaper in the place of worship. They never went out into the real world and everything was brought into them from outside.

The police informed us and we continued to take care of you as if you were our own. You were now known as Helen Taylor and enrolled in the local school in Birdwell. You had difficulty in settling in the school at first and seemed to be withdrawn as if you knew that something was not quite right. Other children talked about their parents and you, according to your teachers seemed to avoid the subject if asked. The other children found it hard to get close to you and so making friends became difficult for you."

"What was my name then, my real name?"

"Mary it was Mary. It is such a lovely name but we were told to change it for your own good."

"Go on Muriel finish the story."

"Well Helen you continued at school I Birdwell and things seemed to beginning to improve. Your teachers told Betty that you were making improvement in all areas including being able to talk about yourself and your family."

"What my real family?"

"No about Betty and John you thought that they were your real family."

Betty sobbed at the thoughts that must be passing through the mind of Helen at that moment. Totally confusing to anyone stood outside never mind when it was you they were talking about.

"Well Betty and John began to feel better then something changed and changed very quickly. Somehow no one knows how it happened but they found out about you and where you had come from. Someone said that a young policeman not thinking of the consequences had blurted it out and it had been overheard. You see many of the communities had to move about as the pits closed one after another. Boys started to bully you and make sounds that you would have no idea what they meant. Parts of Betty and John's home were damaged with what at first looked like small pranks but then they started daubing paint on the gate and walls at the front of the house. 'Scab Lovers'. You tell her Betty."

"We knew what was happening and we also knew that we had to act quickly. We informed the police but they could not do anything without advertising that something was amiss at our home. The social services contacted Muriel and you were rushed away in the dead of night. You must have been frightened to death. Twice in a lifetime taken from people you thought loved you. I know that you would not remember the first but who could know what was in the mind of a child. John and I lived through it for a while but then the damage became more and more and we were accosted in the street. We had to make a decision to move. The council helped by organising a swap for us and we disappeared very much as you had. It was then that we realised that whatever we did however we felt we had to make sure that we did not contact you. I can tell you Helen that we have never suffered more than we suffered at that time.

Helen sat just gazing into her clasped hands. She had just heard the saddest story and a story she never dreamt that she would ever hear. Here were three people that loved her very much and she was sure of that she had been an important part of their lives. She still felt that her childhood had been missed and that although they had been part of it she hadn't felt that they had.

"I just don't know what to say. I feel like I should apologise to you all for my thoughts of these past years and yet I can't. I feel like whoever these people were have cheated me out of what should have been a loving childhood. I should have been able to know my father; hopefully I will still have time to know my mother, my real mother who abandoned me all those years ago.

On the other hand I have met here today two mothers and a father who anyone would be proud to call them their parents, I know that I would."

Everyone took hold of each other and just stood in a circle and hugged each other as the loved flowed from one to the other.

After a while talking turned to the present day and Helen explained what her ambitions were for the future and despite all the early warnings she wanted to visit both Betty and John and Muriel on a regular basis.

Soon the afternoon had gone and Betty and John decided that they had to go. Helen then asked the question that seemed to have been avoided all afternoon.

"Where did I live when I lived with mum and dad?"

Both Betty and Muriel were hoping that this question would not arise but here it was and they knew they would have to answer it.

"Grimethorpe you lived at Grimethorpe and your father was in the Grimethorpe Colliery Brass Band?"

"Grimethorpe you say, do you know that rings a bell with me? Is it too much to ask what my other name was? You told me my first name was Mary what was my second name?"

"Elliot, Mary Elliot."

"Thank you very much for your help Mrs. Taylor and you also Mr. Taylor. Muriel and I will be meeting up again I am sure seeing that we don't live far apart.

I have just remembered why Grimethorpe rings a bell with me. My best friend lived there when she was a child. She is about one year older than I am. She had a tragic life just like me and I think that brought us closer together."

"That is a coincidence Helen. What is her name perhaps we know her?"

"Fields, Joan Fields. Her mother and father were involved in a car crash when she was nine, I think. Anyway her mother was killed outright and her father is a cripple but he's in a home I'm afraid he has given up, on life. Such a pity she is such a nice girl and a really good friend."

Betty and John felt deep shock but did their best to cover it up in front of Helen.

They left the house and when they were out of earshot Betty turned to John.

"You know what family Helen is talking about don't you?"

"Yes love I do. That father of her friend was the one blamed for driving Helen's father to commit suicide. He was the one that drove us from our home. What are we going to do about that then Betty?"

Muriel and Helen said their goodbyes and Helen made arrangements to visit on the following Sunday. It had been arranged that they would both go over to the Taylor's and pick up any papers that Helen needed like her birth certificate.

Chapter Ten

Helen arrived back at Homelands feeling so excited about what she had learned that afternoon her expectations had surpassed her dreams. She was looking forward to telling Joan that she had also been born in Grimethorpe. They had so much in common more than either had realised when they first met.

Helen could still not believe that she had been born in the same village and she was sure that both Joan's and her families must have known each other. Of course she was too young to remember anyone that lived there but just the fact that they had come from the same community was exciting.

Helen was thinking as she walked into the building Joan would not relate to the fact that they were perhaps neighbours because as yet she was unaware of my real name. How silly it had been to take the true identity of a young baby and give it some new name. Yes they had their reasons but surely changing a name was a little bit over the top. Helen went straight to Mrs. Freeman's office to let her know that she had returned from her meeting with her foster parents. Mrs. Freeman called her in and was desperate to find out how much Helen had learned about her background. She had been bursting to tell her the facts that she had in her possession but had not dared in case the social services found out. Confidentiality was so important and the breaking of that could have cost Mrs. Freeman her job.

"Come in Helen tell me how did your meeting with your foster parents go. I do hope you got some satisfaction out of it. I know that you felt very nervous and anxious about the meeting before you left here."

"Oh it was fantastic Mrs. Freeman absolutely fantastic. I can't tell you the relief that I now feel about the whole thing. Oh yes I was nervous, no I was terrified about the meeting. You know so were the Taylor's and Muriel."

"Muriel. Who is that then?"

"Mrs. Hackforth she has been a brick for me you know. I don't know what I would have done without her help."

Helen noted at that moment a frown slide across the face of Mrs. Freeman's, just for a moment but it was there.

"I know that the two most important people in my life at the present moment are you and Mrs. Hackforth. Without you two I would still be wandering around in a mass of don't knows. I want to thank you for your help Mrs. Freeman I know that it has been very difficult for you and that you had your hands tied by the law of the land."

"Thank you Helen it has been very difficult for me but I knew that your determination would shine through for you. I was only too pleased to try and direct you without actually breaking the law.

Now then what did you find out from your foster parents?"

"Everything, well almost I still need to go and see others but at least now I know who they are and that will be very helpful for me."

"You say that you know everything?"

"Yes I know about my father and why he committed suicide and about my mother and how she abandoned me on the steps of that castle in Barnsley."

"Yes but you say that you know about them but what is it that you know?"

"Well my father was driven to suicide by my grandfather well that is what I think happened. Really though it was the strike. Did you know that the miners tried to take on the Government but they lost? Everyone was starving and some had to go to work but the others didn't like it. They fought in the streets and painted things on the walls of the houses. They told me that it was terrible and that families fell out with each other. Were you involved with this Mrs. Freeman?"

"No Helen I was not but everyone knew about it. The television and the papers were constantly featuring it and you could not get away from it. I did feel for all those families and their struggle to survive. The children like you were the main sufferers throughout the strike. I didn't agree with it and I didn't like what the Government was doing to these communities. Communities that had come through a World War taking care of each other whatever the needs had been. Then this thing comes along and breaks all that spirit. I still think that the damage was deeper than anyone realised because it still exists today ten years on."

"Well there is some good news come from it. Joan and I were born in the same village. Yes I can't believe that I made a friend who lived in the same village isn't that strange Mrs. Freeman?"

"Very strange but I say to you take care be prepared for anything."

"What on earth do you mean? Joan is my friend what on earth could I say that would hurt that?" Mrs. Freeman was not sure as to why she had issued her warning. She had no idea if Joan could be a threat to Helen. They were both too young to have known the strike and the animosity that was still hanging about.

"Please just be careful Helen that is all I am telling you. What do you intend to do now then?"

"First of all I want to tell Joan my news and then perhaps tomorrow we may both go back to the village where we were born. I still have family living there my real family not my foster family."

"You mean your real family?"

"Yes my name is not really Helen Taylor it's Mary Elliot. The Taylor's changed it so that I would not be identified; well that is what they told me. The social services apparently thought that I could be in danger and by them looking after me I would place them in danger. I was just a baby how could I hurt them isn't it silly?"

"No it was not at the time Helen. Do you intend to keep your new name or are you thinking of returning back to your old name?"

Helen thought for a moment before she answered. "Do you know I have never thought about it I suppose that I should change back to my birth name I need to find my mother and then I can make that sort of decision. Everyone knew me as Helen so it would be difficult to try and tell them why I have changed my name to Mary, don't you think?"

"I suppose it would. Anyway you will not see Joan today."

"Why where is she?"

"She received news this morning about her father she had to dash off to the hospital."

Helen's face changed from excitement to one of concern.

"Please don't tell me that he died. Poor Joan, no he can't have died. I know that he did not know her but she still had a father."

"No he didn't die in fact he actually spoke for the first time last night. He only spoke a few words but he asked for his wife. Joan told me before she left that the doctors seemed very excitement."

"That is good news it is better news than I have had today. We both have something to be happy about don't we?"

"Yes I think that you have Helen. I expect that you want to freshen up before we all have tea. You have had a busy day and I am so pleased that you have heard the news that you wanted to."

"Yes I am tired and a shower would help to shake off some of that tiredness. Inside I am dancing with excitement. Thank you Mrs. Freeman."

Helen walked over and kissed Mrs. Freeman on the cheek that took her by surprise. She tried to be kind to her girls but yet keep the girls at a distance. This helped the discipline and enabled her to have a better perspective overall on the girl's needs.

Helen left and went to her room. She had her own thoughts but these were constantly interrupted by the thoughts of how Joan must be feeling at that moment.

At the hospital Joan had been joined in the waiting room by two of the doctors that had been taking care of her father. They were telling her about the incident of the previous night and their interpretation of what it could mean.

Joan listened but inside her stomach rolled as the butterflies churned around in there.

She wanted to ask the obvious question but dare not in case the answer was not what she wanted to hear.

The doctors went on and on about the safeguards that they had to take and that Joan should not become too excited by what happened last night. They explained that the mind sometimes wakes like a door opening just for a split second and then closes once again. They told her that no one knew what caused this and research was going on so that everyone could be better informed.

Joan didn't hear half what they were saying she remembered the story that Helen had told her about her Mrs. James and how playing her favourite music seemed to help her.

Her father was a fan of Elvis Presley and she knew that Heartbreak Hotel was the favourite of both her mother and her father.

"Could I play him some music please?"

The doctors looked at Joan as if she had asked if she could take over the case and had prescribed some mysterious new drug.

"We don't see what…

"I have heard that it can help in some cases. Why can't we just try it we have nothing to lose have we?"

The doctors looked at each other and shrugged their shoulders.

"No I suppose not. Go ahead and try bring what you need into the hospital and we will make sure that everyone is aware."

Joan knew that the hospital had its own radio station and had spoken to the local DJ before when she made some requests for music to be played. The DJ was glad to help and made a tape for Joan to enable her to play on her tape recorder.

"Do you need any more Elvis songs Joan I have a big collection of most of his tracks."

"No but just keep repeating Heartbreak Hotel over and over then I do not have to keep rewinding the tape."

Joan returned to the ward where her father lay and started to play the tape. The DJ had managed to get twelve repeats so Joan could just sit there and watch her father looking for any movement from the eyes or mouth. Nothing happened and Joan sat there for the next four hours rewinding the tape on three occasions. Joan was a lover of Elvis because she had been brought up with it but after four hours of the same song was a little too much even for her. She decided that she would turn off the tape and just sit talking had she had done on many occasions and for many hours in the past.

One of the doctors came to see her it was going on for ten o'clock that evening but Joan had never noticed the passage of time.

"I think that you would be better if you went home and have some rest Joan."

"I would like to stay if that would be possible I want to be here if he wakes again. I know that you will understand doctor."

"Yes I can understand Joan but I cannot say that your father will wake up again. There are no guarantees not in this game."

"I do understand but I still want to be here. Please make that possible for me."

The doctor shook his head. "I will arrange that for you but please don't allow the state of your father make you ill hat will serve no purpose, no purpose at all."

"No I won't do that I promise you."

Joan spent the night in a small side room close to the ward. These rooms were specific for such an arrangement but comfort was not one of the properties of these rooms. Nurses and doctors during late shifts sometimes used these rooms.

It was becoming light through a small window when a nurse disturbed Joan and asked her to go with her. Joan rubbed her eyes and was not totally awake but slipped her trousers on and followed the nurse out and into the ward where her father lay.

"What is it, nurse?"

"Take a look your father's eyes are open."

Joan moved over to the side of the bed and leaned over her father so she was in his eyesight.

"Hello dad…."

"Annie is that you?"

"No dad it's Joan. You have been asleep welcome back."

He licked his lips and Joan picked up a cup of water but the nurse stopped her.

"He needs a drink nurse."

"Yes I know but just wet this and wipe his lips he may choke if you give him a drink like that."

"Sorry nurse I didn't think."

Joan wiped the cloth across his lips and it was obvious how much he was enjoying the coolness on his lips.

"Thank you Annie you always take care of me don't you?"

"No dad I am your daughter Joan, I have been waiting for you."

"Joan you say yes I did have a daughter called Joan."

"Yes that is me dad."

Tears ran down her cheeks as her father tried to move his eyes across her face trying to recognise her. His eyes searched her and the expression on his face began to slowly change. The doctor joined Joan and took hold of her father's hand and took his pulse. He listened to his chest to make sure that the heartbeat was normal.

"Is everything all right doctor is he alright?"

"Yes he's fine but we must keep him calm so don't press him just do what you have been doing for all those weeks. Let him come back in his own time Joan. I know that you feel excited but it is your father who is the important person in this room."

"Yes I know that doctor."

Joan spent the following day just talking about old times excluding the trip to Blackpool. She decided that this could bring back the death of her mother that had caused her father to drift into his state in the first place.

It was going on for teatime when Joan was taken aback. Her father speech had been improving all that day with the constant wiping of his lips with the moist cloth.

"I've been with your mother you know. I was walking with Annie I thought that you were Annie. You have her eyes and her mouth. She is happy you know and says that we have not to worry. I made a lot of mistakes in the past and Annie has told me how to put them right. I hurt a lot of people and I am so sorry about that."

"A lot of people made mistakes dad. No one is perfect and we have to put things right whenever that is possible."

"Annie, your mother never made mistakes she was a saint you know. I was the head of the house but your mother was the boss. I should have listened to her instead of going mad all those people that lost their jobs because of me."

"No dad it was not your fault it was how it was then. Anyone would have done what you did you thought that you were right."

"Your mam didn't think so. I tore her apart you know some of her best friends she had to support me like she always did. She supported me even when she knew that I was wrong. She turned her back of friends that she had grown up with. Her faith in me was too much but I knew that I could always rely on her backing she was always faithful to me. I didn't deserve that no one deserves that sort of loyalty from anyone."

"The strike was bigger than you though dad and you did your best, no one can hold that against you."

"No Joan your mother is right I need to make my peace with everyone. I hurt some people too much and I can't put that right but I can only try."

"Dad you called me Joan."

"Well that is your name isn't it? I am not daft you know perhaps I have been in the past but your mother has put that right. She reckons that I was cursed by someone but I don't believe in that sort of thing."

"Cursed whatever are you talking about dad? Who would wish to place a curse on you?"

"I can think of a few people love. I did bad things to people that I once called my friends and we played in the band together for years. No I did a great deal of harm and I do hope that God can forgive me for my sins."

"I am sure that he will dad he will know that you were only acting on your beliefs and thinking of your fellow men at that time."

"No love I thought that I was but evil entered my thoughts and the devil took over my thinking."

The doctor took hold of Joan's shoulder.

"I think that we should allow your father to have a little nap Joan. You can come back this afternoon we need to make some more tests just to make sure."

"But he seems…

"Yes he is but we don't want, you know what I am saying."

"Yes doctor. I am going dad but I will be back later now don't you be going out and leave the nurses alone while I am away."

Joan's father managed a small but weary smile."

Joan's heart was beating faster and faster when she began to realise that there was a good probability that she was actually getting her father back.

Helen waited anxiously for Joan to return so that she could tell her about the good news she had learned during her visit to Mrs. Hackforth's.

Helen went along to see if Mrs. Freeman had heard any news from Joan. She had been away almost three days now and Helen fearing the worst, thinking that perhaps Joan's father had died. Inside her stomach churned if he had lost her father how could she tell her about her exciting news?

Helen decided that she would go to Grimethorpe and try to contact her grandmother Mrs. Taylor had told her that she still lived in the village. She sat on the end of her bed wondering how she would be received after all of this time. She could not remember what her grandmother looked like so how would she know that she was talking to the right woman.

Still she thought I have come so far now I cannot turn back I must go forward. Helen told Mrs. Freeman what she was planning and though Mrs. Freeman was a little worried she knew that Helen would go anyway.

"Just take your time and do not try and rush in with both feet Helen. Remember that you were just a baby when you left there. If you go in expecting that your grandmother will take you in her arms and hug you, well she may after a while. Just be sensible that is all the advice that I can give you."

"Thank you Mrs. Freeman I know what you mean. I feel very nervous and apprehensive about the whole visit but it is a thing that I have to do. I need to know what happened to my mother. I need to know whether she is alive or dead so that I can come to terms within myself. I hope that you can try and understand what I am saying."

"I do understand Helen and I hope to God that everything turns out right for you. I have been praying for you over the past weeks. Praying that you don't come to any harm and you find whatever it is that you seek."

"Thank you Mrs. Freeman I appreciate that. I have done a great deal of praying myself so perhaps between us we may have done some good."

Joan set off in her small car for Grimethorpe it would take her about thirty minutes or so to get there depending on the traffic. The journey was one of solemn thoughts trying to sort out how she would approach her grandmother and how she could break the news that she actually was. The last thing she wanted was to frighten and perhaps give her grandmother a heart attack by just turning up on the doorstep.

Finally she entered the village it was much bigger than she thought and although she knew roughly where her grandmother lived she had not got the number.

Helen decided to call in at the post office and enquire there. The young woman that stood behind the counter was busily talking to someone when Helen approached. Helen stood and waited but it was obvious that they were talking about something that had happened to someone in the village. It was nothing to do with the shopping but Helen thought that was what village life was about. They were not being nosy just enquiring about someone, anyone.

Finally the other woman left and the young woman turned her attention to Helen.

"Yes love what can I do for you?"

"I was wondering if you could direct me to my… to Mrs. Elliot's house?"

"Mrs. Elliot eh she doesn't get many visitors these days. You are not from around here are you?"

"No I live in Doncaster I am just trying to find Mrs. Elliot if you could help me please."

"Mary….

"Yes."

Then Helen realised that she was not talking about her.

"Is that your name then? Mary."

"No my name is Helen Taylor."

The young woman looked strangely at Helen. "Why did you answer yes for then when I was talking about Mrs. Elliot?"

"I have no idea I suppose it was some sort of reaction. I just don't know could you tell me…

"Of course I can Helen. When you leave the shop turn the next corner and you will see two houses standing alone. Mary's is the first one. She refused to move when they wanted to knock down the rest of the row, she is a bit of a stickler is our Mary. Nobody from the council will knock her about."

Helen thanked the young woman and just wanted to get out of that shop before she had had to tell her all about herself before she had left the shop. There was no doubt that this young woman was the very person that took in all the gossip and passed it along through those in the village. She would be the one that would probably find out after her visit to her grandmother's house.

Helen turned the corner and spotted the two houses that the young woman had spoken of. Either side of the two houses were mounds of brick rubble where the other houses had been knocked down to make space for something or other thought up by the councillors.

Helen decoded that she had to march straight up to the front door without any hesitation and knock and hope for the best. Dithering about would just make things worse.

On the outside she may have looked brave but inside her stomach was churning over and over with nervous twitches.

Helen knocked on the old front door. It seemed a lifetime before she heard the bolt being pulled back and the door open.

There before her stood a small but erect standing old lady. A quick estimate suggested that she would be in her late sixties or early seventies.

"Yes what can I do for you? You are not from the council are you?"

Helen was taken aback she had rehearsed how she was going to approach this point of the contact with her grandmother.

"No I am not from the council. My name is Helen Taylor. I think that you may be my grandmother."

The old ladies face frowned as she was hit with this suggestion by someone she didn't know standing there on her front step. She was expecting someone from the council and here she was facing someone who says that she may be her grandchild."

"Excuse me love, but why do you think that I may be your grandmother?"

"I have been searching for my relatives for some months now. I found my many foster parents and from them I traced you. My name is Mary Elliot…

"You just told me that it was Helen Taylor so how is it that you are now calling yourself Mary Elliot.

You know that Mary Elliot is my name is there some coincidence?"

"No my father was James Elliot and my mother's name was Florence....

The old lady started to stagger on her feet. Helen took hold of her to steady her before she fell.

"Can we go inside and sit down?"

Her grandmother nodded at that moment she was speechless.

Helen took her in the front room and sat her down on the large settee that seemed to take up most of the space in the room.

"I am so sorry if I have upset you but I could not think of a way that could have eased the way that I told you. I know how you must feel I know how I felt when I found out."

The old lady shook her head and held out her hand in a gesture for Helen to take hold of it.

"I can see that you are your mother's daughter now my love. Why did it take you so long to find me I knew that you existed but whatever I did to try and find you I failed? No one would tell me anything about you or where you were. I did find out that your mother had given you up but she would not tell anyone to whom. She was so frightened that someone would hurt you even though I tried to tell her that this was nonsense."

"You have seen my mother then? How is she? Will I be able to see her?"

"My goodness what a lot of questions yes just after my husband, your grandfather, died I tried my best to find your mother I knew that she had been desperate but the police had failed to find her. Then I found out that a baby had been found on the steps of the National Union of Mineworkers Offices. I had a strong feeling that it was our child because you mother blamed the union for the death of your father, my son."

"Why, why did father commit suicide? I want to try and understand how a father could leave his wife and baby to fend for themselves."

The old lady started to cry and Helen took hold of her.

"I am so sorry to upset you but I need to know."

Sobbing through her handkerchief she nodded her head.

"I know you do love and I would tell you if I truly understood. I don't know how much you know about that time in our lives the most terrible time when everyone became like animals. Friends turning their backs but worse still were that whole families broke up in a sea of hate. Your grandfather was a good man who helped people without a second thought. He seemed to change overnight after it became obvious that they were losing the war. He was not a militant man he was just a caring man. He didn't become a major part of the union to seek power. In fact it was his many friends that persuaded him so that he could take care of their needs."

"But he drove my father, his son out. Surely he knew that my father was just looking to support his family including a young baby, your grandchild."

"Yes, yes that is all true but he became under so much pressure from mobs of people and he could not be seen to support one without supporting similar people…

"But this was his son, his own flesh and blood. How could any human being treat people like that whether they were related or not?"

"I have asked myself that question on so many occasions the fact that he had taken this stand proved to be very dear. It cost your grandfather his life in the end. I lost a son and a dear husband so yes I have asked myself that question on so many occasions. The media looked at the losses in the mining industry but no one gave us a second thought. I had to try and find your mother to try and make things right between us. We had both lost everything that we loved and I had to try and put that right whatever the cost.

I fought them all when they came banging on our door demanding that Eli do something about the 'Scabs' that were still living in the village. He constantly cried in his sleep, he was too proud to do it in front of me. These were his so-called friends that had begged him to take this job. They didn't do anything to help him they just gave him trouble. They even attacked our home.

I knew how my son must have felt when they attacked your home he was thinking that if he died then the trouble would die with him. I could understand but that was a useless death caused by a strike that helped no one."

"Did they try and hurt my mother and me then?"

"Some young people became obsessed because of what their fathers had suffered but they never did it in the open. They would do things under the cover of darkness and so many people were frightened it is a wonder that many others didn't do the same.

When your father committed suicide your grandfather became very depressed and shouted at the youths of the village about their antics. He had no idea who the culprits were, so he blanket covered them all. They then started to turn on him and he just couldn't take anymore from his so-called friends. He went out one night telling me that he was going round to try and stop the trouble in the community but he never came back. I stayed up all night and I feared for his safety. I called the police, who despite the problems that we had caused them came to see me. They knew that some of their own relatives were involved with the dispute so they didn't hold any grudges against us. They searched the village and found your grandfather hanging from the same tree that your father had died....

Again things became too much and she broke down. Helen hugged her and kissed her forehead. "I am so sorry for putting you all this grandmother shall I make a cup of tea for us perhaps it will help?"

A nod from her grandmother sent Helen into the kitchen.

"What happened to your neighbours, grandma?" Helen was thinking that if she changed the subject it would help ease the upset that the recent conversation had caused her.

"The council took their homes they wanted mine but I was not going to allow them to bulldoze me out like they did my neighbours."

"Bulldoze, how did they do that?"

"Well three of them rented the properties but some of us had bought them. We, that is your grandfather and I, we spent a lot of money upgrading ours when we bought it. The council offered us next to nothing. I took them to court but they still try and outwit me. That is why I thought that you could have been sent to try and soften me. I tell you I have too many fond memories to allow them to cheat me."

"They look to have tried to demoralise you by demolishing the house around you. It must be hard to look out there at what used to be your friendly neighbours homes."

"It is and I have no doubt they will win but like your grandfather I will not give up without a fight."

"Well as long as it does not lead to what happened to him. I want to get to know you I have lost eighteen years of my life. Where did you say that my mother was staying?"

Helen joined her back in the lounge carrying the pot of tea and two cups.

"I didn't tell you… Come on sit down love. I am afraid that I have bad news for you. Yes even more, we both could do with something to laugh about.

I am afraid that I did manage to find your mother after months and months of trying. The police helped me, as did the Missing Persons. I can remember the day that the police came around to the house. I had barred the door just in case the council came around. After a while they convinced me that they were here with news about your mother.

They told me that she had been admitted to the hospital in Sheffield. This was strange because we thought that she could be in Bradford because I knew that she had relatives there.

Anyway I went over to Sheffield and she was very poorly. They had found her wandering the streets wet through and looking very ill. I just stood and cried knowing that we had been part of the conspiracy that had driven a lovely family woman to this."

"Well is she all right now?"

"No love she isn't…

"Tell me, what happened to her?"

"She died love. She had cancer in her breast but she had left it too late. The doctors tried but they knew that they were fighting a losing battle. She was very weak and the growth had spread throughout her body. I can still see that sad looking lady laid there in that bed. I resolved the situation on my own mind that at least she was joining the man that she loved very much. They were so devoted your father and mother you know."

"I wish that I could have known them. I would have loved to know my father they say that girls always love their father."

"That is true Helen or should I call you Mary? You know that my name is Mary don't you? Your mother insisted that you were called after me and I was so proud of that."

"Yes I did know the young lady in the post office told me when I was asking where you lived."

"You mean Barbara I bet she tried to probe you when you asked her."

"She did I thought that she would need to be told my whole life story before she would tell me where you lived."

"Tell me about your foster parents did they look after you?"

Helen then went through how she stayed with the Taylor's and how they changed her name and then had to move because of the troubles then how she moved to the Hackforth's and then the James's. Finally telling her about Homelands and how she had started to look for her parents and how Mrs. Freeman had helped her get started.

"What about boyfriends then Mary. A lovely young lady like you must have them going mad to have a date?"

Helen didn't correct her grandmother when she called her Mary but it felt so strange after eighteen years to not be called Helen.

"No I have not had time for boys we don't have them at Homelands. I have a good friend that I met at Homelands. I am waiting to see her because all the time that we have been friends we had not realised that we came from the same village. Her father is very ill in hospital and she is with him at the moment. I can't wait to tell her when I get back."

"She came from here did she? What is her name perhaps I know the family?"

"Fields, Joan Fields."

"Fields, did her mother get killed in a car crash?"

"Yes that's them. Did you know them then?"

"Oh yes I knew them. We were friends at one time. Her husband was badly injured and he came back here to live for a few years after the accident but he never settled. They say that he was losing his mind. They had a little girl and I think that she was taken into care."

"Yes she was. Her father drifted into a coma and they thought that he could die. I think that he may have because they sent for Joan the other day and I have not seen her since."

"So he should. He was one of the main reasons that your father killed himself. The rumour in the village is that someone placed a curse on him and that was the cause of the accident but it killed the wrong person."

Helen's face said it all. Her best friend's father killed her father and as a consequence, her mother. How could she? Anger exploded inside her and hate friendship was quickly turning to hate.

"It was not your friend's fault she was like you an innocent party in all this."

At the hospital Joan had returned to talk to her father. He was looking much brighter and he had become more talkative and his speech had become much clearer and distinctive.

"Hello dad you really look a lot better. How do you feel inside I know these have been trying times for you losing mum like we did. But you have to come to terms with that you have a daughter, a daughter who loves you very much."

Joan could see a tear forming in his eyes. She had been told by the doctor to take things slowly and at her father's speed.

"Losing your mum was the worst thing that could have happened to me. I was totally lost I had no idea where the future lay."

"But I was still alive dad. I needed you I lost a mum as much as you lost a wife. I felt like you had both deserted me when I needed you the most. I was nine years of age and I had no one, no one at all to help me."

"I know love and I can see that now but what with the strike and the friends I lost there and then your mother it was more than anyone could take. I know that I had you but I just could not face a future without your mother. It is important that you understand what I am saying to you. It was not that I didn't love you but could I do for you what your mother could, I couldn't see that. I had to allow you to find another outlet and that was your auntie. I knew that I was growing away from the real world into a world that made me feel comfortable."

"I didn't have that comfort zone dad. I wandered through my early years not knowing where that journey was taking me."

"I know and I will try and make that right but it will not be easy. I have another important thing to do. A thing that if I do not put right I will have no future my conscience will now allow me to have a normal life. I know that I will never walk properly again but they have told me that I can become mobile and I know that there are many more people worse off than me."

"What is it that is so important for you to sort out?"

"Some of the families that my actions caused great stress and a lot more unhappiness I don't think that they will forgive me but I have to try. I will need you to help me with this task Joan."
"But how can I help you I don't know who these people are?"
"No but you can start the ball rolling for me. I need to see them but in my state that would be impossible. I need you to visit and ask not beg them if they will come and see me. I have to make my peace with these people. They were my friends and I let the strike take over that friendship. I didn't just lose the war I lost so many friends along the way friends that would not have done the same thing to me.
"You know that my best friend committed suicide because of me. How would you feel if a thing like that was on your conscience Joan, could you live with that?"

"No I don't think that I could father but if he is dead what can you do to help him and you?"

"His family he had a family. They left the village after that fateful day to escape the wrath that we had bestowed just because they saw things differently to us. Will you do that for me Joan? I know you felt that I deserted you and you would be right to think that but I need you like I have never needed anyone before. If you don't help me I don't know what I….

"I will help you dad. You know that whatever you did I don't feel angry with you and I am sure that those that you speak of will find it in their hearts to forgive you."

"I hope that you are right but this is deep and many of those who we hurt are still suffering the consequences of those actions. You know there are many out there that still think those actions were right and may never ever forgive. The heart of my community was torn out and that can never be replaced despite any sorrow that we may feel. I have to make my peace as much as I can."

"All right then dad but have you some names and addresses that will enable me to start and look?"

"Yes love I have. The first and probably the most important are the Elliot's in Grimethorpe. Jimmy Elliot was my best friend and we played in the brass band together for so many years. We even went to school together and he actually saved me from drowning in the local canal. I managed to turn his family into the most hated family in the village simply because he was my friend and I felt he had let me down badly. I even turned his father and mother against him so much so he finished up committing suicide and leaving a wife and small baby."

"You mean that his father and mother turned their backs on their own son and grand baby? That is so terrible they ought to be cursed never mind you.

Turning you back on your own family, it is just unbelievable I am speechless."

"That was what they did to us. That Government did all that to us they turned us into animals with no human emotions. We have to put that right and never allow it to happen again. They paid the price in the end just like I did. I have the prospect of trying to put what I did right, they can't Jimmy's father also committed suicide after he realised what he had done to his family."

"Well I am pleased that you didn't commit suicide dad whatever you did. I need a father. I need to learn to know you like a daughter should know her father."

"Thank you love I don't deserve you but I promise you that I have no intentions of leaving you again. We will get to know each other and perhaps your friend, Helen, was that her name? Perhaps she will come and see me sometime. I would like to meet her she must be special if she is a friend of yours. "

"Yes I am sure she will dad. She is special and we have so much in common. She is trying to find her family but she is worse off than I was. I knew where you were so even though you were asleep I had a father of some sort. She has nothing and she is trying to find people who can help her discover who she is."

"Poor lass she must have had a hard life."

"Yes dad but I bet you when I ask her to help me with what you want me to do she will drop everything and help me."

"That is a true friend Joan so you take great care of her. I gave up my friends and for what? I can tell you something Joan we should always appreciate a good friend. To give them up as easily as I did then I don't deserve to have any. So listen to me you take good care of her."

Joan made her way to Grimethorpe to try and start her father's wishes to try and put right the wrongs that he felt he had done.

Joan knew where the Elliot's lived unless of course they had moved since her days living in the village. Knocking on the door it was opened by Helen. They just stared at each other with mouths open wide. After a few minutes of shock and surprise Helen spoke.

"Joan what on earth are you doing here? How did you know where to find me?"

"I didn't I am here on behalf of my father He sent me to see Mrs. Elliot. What are you doing here I didn't know that you knew Mrs. Elliot?"

"She's my grandmother and I came looking for you to tell you but you had been called to see your father. You say that he asked you to come here does that mean he is feeling all right?"

"Yes he is out of the coma and he actually remembers me."

"That is great Joan I am so pleased for you. I didn't realise that your family knew my grandmother.

Then you did say that you came from Grimethorpe if I remember right."

"Yes I told you."

"Then your family must have known my family because they have lived in the village according to my grandmother for years. Didn't you tell me that your father played in the Colliery Brass Band?"

"Yes, that's right he did for many years until his accident."

"So did my father they must have known each other. Isn't it a small world?"

Suddenly Helen heard her grandmother calling from the front room.

"Who is it dear?"

"It's my friend Joan she has come to see you."

"Joan. Joan, who is she?"

"Joan Fields she is here to see you apparently her father has sent her."

"You had better bring her through."

Helen took Joan through into the lounge but the face of her grandmother was not showing any sort of welcome at all.

"What is it that you want what could your father want to say to me what could be significant. It seems that he cannot come and see me himself he has to send his daughter."

"No, no you don't understand he is still very ill in hospital he will be coming when he can walk when the hospital allow him to leave."

"Hospital he should be in the cemetery not in the hospital he killed my husband and killed my son."

Helen looked at her grandmother once again with the look of shock written all over it.

"You are saying that Joan's father was the one that killed my father and ultimately the life of my grandfather."

"Yes he was so intent to break the government he and his confederates ruined this community and the families that lived here."

"But he's changed Mrs. Elliot he has changed and he wants to make things right. He knows that what he did was so wrong turning his back on his friends and neighbours. Don't forget my grandfather was killed down the mine is it not surprising that he should want the best for the people he represented."

Joan could not believe the words that were coming out of her mouth. Her father had not told her to say these words they were coming from her heart.

"What brought about this change, this search for forgiveness?"

"He believes that he has spoken to mother…

"Annie well there was a lovely woman. Your father almost killed her before the accident with his principles. He was so principled but had no room for any sentiment for anyone except himself."

Joan could not hold back the tears anymore but only Helen showed any concern for the feelings of her friend.

"I am so sorry Helen but you know that I had no idea, we were so young then how could we have changed anything we can't be blamed for our father's mistakes."

"No Joan you are right and I am not blaming you. I think that your father was wrong to send you but then I believe that I would have done the same thing."

Helen's grandmother listened intently whilst the two girls were talking and inside she knew that Helen was right. The young ones had nothing to do with what happened in those days. The older generation should try and show some compassion and allow the younger ones to try and resurrect the community spirit.

"Joan comes here love I am sorry that I showed you, well I am sorry. Your mother and I were really good friends and we both backed our husbands in the fight even though we both thought that it went too far.

Your father like my husband, Helen's grandfather, tore this community apart and along with it their families. I remember you when you were a baby but I did not have the pleasure of seeing my grandchild. Helen here was taken away from me. That is something that I will find hard to forgive and I will never forget."

Helen's grandmother took hold of Joan and comforted her until the tears subsided.

"I am sorry for what my father did Mrs. Elliot and I do believe that his sorrow is genuine. He believes that he had a curse placed on him by someone. He thinks that he lost his wife, my mother, due to the curse. Do you know if someone did this to my family Mrs. Elliot?"

"No but I could think of a few who would have gladly done so if they had the power. Those times were bad, really bad. I don't know if it is at all possible but finding that old community spirit is so important if happiness is to return to these villages.

It will be up to your generation to try and find it and bring it back."

"I know what you mean Mrs. Elliot but I don't think that the young ones like Helen and I have the skill to find it. You have to remember that most of those villagers had the common problem of hard and dangerous work and they had gone through the Second World War. The apprenticeship that we had does not give us that sort of skill."

Helen was impressed by what Joan had just said and agreed with her sentiments completely.

"Come on let's all have a cup of tea. We need to try and understand where it is your father is coming from. I think that it will take a bit more than a visit by yourself Joan even though you are a lovely girl and you have your mother's looks."

"That was what my father said when he opened his eyes from the coma. He called me Annie and that was a bit of a shock."

"I bet it was but I am glad for you sake that your father is getting well. Every girl needs to know their father."

"Yes I wish I had known my father."

Joan and her grandmother placed their arms around Helen and they all hugged each other. Helen had found her family and her grandmother had the grandchild that she lost but more importantly Joan and Helen had still remained good friends.

The End

Printed in Great Britain
by Amazon